Meg Began Jogging over the Wet Pavement Toward Home.

She realized it must have rained again while she was at Shannon's, for the street was very wet and currents of water were rolling down the curbsides toward the sewers.

She looked up and saw headlights and then a dark car behind them. It was coming toward her very fast, its tires splashing up waves of rainwater on both sides as it moved.

Keeping to the curb, Meg continued to jog. But she froze in place when she realized that the car had swerved so that it was coming right at her.

It seemed to speed up.

She had no time to move, no time to jump out of its path.

Frozen like a frightened deer, she tossed up her hands as if to shield herself, and screamed as the car roared down on her.

The Surprise Party

R.L. STINE

AN ARCHWAY PAPERBACK
Published by POCKET BOOKS
New York   London   Toronto   Sydney   Tokyo   Singapore

This book is a work of fiction. Names, characters, places and incidents are either the product of the author's imagination or are used fictitiously. Any resemblance to actual events or locales or persons, living or dead, is entirely coincidental.

AN ARCHWAY PAPERBACK *Original*

An Archway Paperback published by
POCKET BOOKS, a division of Simon & Schuster Inc.
1230 Avenue of the Americas, New York, NY 10020

ISBN: 0-671-73561-6

First Archway Paperback printing August 1989

10 9 8 7 6 5 4

AN ARCHWAY PAPERBACK and colophon are
registered trademarks of Simon & Schuster Inc.

FEAR STREET is a registered trademark of
Parachute Press.

Printed in the U.S.A.

IL 7+

The, Surprise Party

prologue

*H*ow easy it was. And how quick.

The rifle popped, cracked like a cheap firecracker.

Bye-bye, Evan.

Pleasant dreams.

It was so easy. And not all that unpleasant, really. Especially if you didn't think about it.

Especially if you locked the whole picture up in some remote corner of your mind—and thought instead about . . . her.

She was so baad.

How else could he describe her? He thought about her all the time. She was always invading his brain, pushing away what he was supposed to be thinking about, until sometimes he thought she might drive him crazy, really crazy.

He would do anything, he realized, for her.

She was so baad. He wanted to crush her, crush her, crush her. He wanted her to be with him, to care only for him, to feel just the way he did.

And now she would.

He wiped the rifle handle off against his shirt and walked quickly along the path through the trees.

The woods were quiet, so quiet now.

Everything was so fresh and leafy green. Everything was so bright and cheerful.

He started to walk more quickly, his boots crunching loudly over dry twigs and weeds. He turned and took one last look at the body.

Would he get away with it?

Of course he would. . . .

chapter

1

*M*eg Dalton pressed the handbrakes and skidded her bike to a stop on the dirt path. She took a deep breath and smiled. "Sure smells like spring," she said.

Sunlight filtered through the tall trees, with their fresh, green leaves still unfurling. Dogwoods and cherry trees were already in bloom, blanketing Shadyside Park with splashes of white and pink.

It's so beautiful here in May. It's like riding through a fairy-tale world, Meg thought. Her friends were always putting her down for saying things like that. She decided to keep the thought to herself.

Her two companions, pedaling their bikes leisurely, caught up to her. "Hey, Meg—why'd you stop?" Tony called.

"Let's keep going to the river," Shannon said, gliding past Meg, then turning around. "Come on. I want to ride. I've got to burn off some of the extra pounds I put on this winter."

Meg stared at her friend. Shannon didn't have any extra pounds to take off. Her figure was perfect. With her coppery hair, blue eyes, and full, pouty mouth, Meg thought, Shannon looked just like that actress in the movies, Molly Ringwald.

"I've gotta get a new bike," Tony said. "There's no rubber left on the pedals."

"Ssshhhh," Meg interrupted, pointing to a bed of pink and purple wildflowers just ahead. "Look. A hummingbird."

"Are we gonna keep riding, or what?" Shannon asked impatiently. "If I knew this was going to be a nature field trip, I would've brought my notebook."

Shannon hopped back on her bike seat and pedaled away. Meg hurried to catch up to her. "Hey—wait up!" Tony called. "It's hard to pedal with no rubber on the pedals!"

They rode past a noisy softball game on the public diamond, recognizing several of their friends from Shadyside High. In the sloping, grassy field beyond the diamond, people were sunning themselves, throwing Frisbees, and having picnics.

It's like everyone has burst out of their cocoons and come out ready for fun, Meg thought. She knew her friends would put her down for that thought, too.

Everyone was always teasing Meg for being too gung ho, too enthusiastic, too bright and chirpy. She was short and, to her constant regret, still hadn't developed much of a figure. And with her round face, short blond hair, and big blue eyes, she was sometimes mistaken for a kid, which drove her bananas!

A baby squirrel scampered across the path, and Meg

had to swerve to miss it. "That could've been five points!" Tony called from several yards behind.

"Not funny, Tony," Meg called back. She pedaled harder and caught up to Shannon.

"Tony seems to be in a good mood," Shannon said, her eyes straight ahead on the path.

"He's done nothing but complain about his bike the whole afternoon," Meg said with a sigh.

"But for *him*, that's being in a good mood!" Shannon cracked.

Meg forced a laugh. She realized that Shannon was right about Tony. He had been so moody all winter. He was always losing his temper and getting angry for the tiniest reasons, or for no reason at all.

At first Meg thought maybe it was her fault. Maybe Tony was getting tired of her. They had been going together for more than two years. Maybe he was angry because he wanted to dump her and didn't know how. But every time she mentioned it, he got a hurt look on his face and swore that nothing was wrong.

The ground grew soft as the path began to lower itself toward the river. They had to pedal around deep puddles of rain water.

"And how are you and Dwayne getting along?" Meg teased. It was the only thing she could ever think of to tease Shannon about.

"That creep!" Shannon shouted, breathing hard from her rapid pedaling. "He follows me around like a sick puppy, with those dark, mournful eyes. Ugh. He's always flexing his muscles in those tight white T-shirts he wears, you know, showing off."

"Well, he works out all the time. He's really got a great bod," Meg said.

Shannon looked surprised. That was such an un-Meg thing to say. "Well, he's still a creep. He's always hanging out with your cousin Brian, playing *Wizards and Dungeons* in the woods. Oh—" Shannon suddenly realized what she had said. "I didn't mean to say that your cousin is a creep. I—"

"That's okay. Brian is definitely a little weird," Meg said, laughing.

There didn't seem to be any more to say. They rode on for a long while in silence. Meg felt a sudden chill, more from her thoughts than from the wind. It was exactly a year ago, she realized. Exactly a year ago that Brian had found Shannon's brother Evan.

Exactly a year ago on a spring day just like this one that Brian had found Evan—shot to death in the Fear Street woods.

Meg shook her head as if to shake away the memory.

At least Shannon can laugh now, Meg found herself thinking. At least she can crack jokes again and go biking in the park with her old friends.

What a long winter.

Meg slowed down and let Tony catch up. "How's it goin', slowpoke?"

"I think my chain's slipping," he grumbled. He pulled off the maroon sweatshirt he'd been wearing, revealing a gray T-shirt underneath, and tied the sweatshirt around his waist. Despite the cool winds off the river, he was sweating. "I've gotta get a new bike," he said, climbing off and bending down to inspect the chain.

She loved the way he looked when he studied something closely, the way his dark eyebrows lowered and his forehead wrinkled, his frown of concentration. "You'll be working for your dad as soon as school's out," Meg said. "You'll be able to save up for a new bike."

"Yeah, sure," he muttered, wiping his grease-covered hand on his jeans. "With what the old man's paying me to pump gas, maybe I can afford a pogo stick." He climbed back on the bike and started to pedal away.

She followed along the curving path. Beyond a long field of tall grass and reeds, the narrow, brown Conononka River flowed quickly but silently, high on its banks, since there had been a lot of snow that winter. Meg was surprised to see Shannon down by the river at the end of the bike path, talking to two other kids on bikes.

As she rode closer, Meg recognized Lisa Blume and Cory Brooks. Lisa and Cory had become something of a joke around Shadyside High. They had grown up next door to each other and were lifelong friends. The previous winter they had started dating—and ever since, they hadn't been able to get along at all!

Tony and Meg rode up to meet them. "We were just heading back," Cory said. "It's cold down here."

"What are you two doing tonight?" Shannon asked Lisa.

"I don't know. Cory didn't make any plans," Lisa said with the wry half-sneer that often crossed her face. "I don't think he remembered we had a date."

"I thought we'd just hang out or something," Cory said uncomfortably. He started to put his arm around Lisa, but she stepped away.

"Tony and I aren't going out," Meg said. "I've got

7

to stay home and work on my final report for psych. I am so far behind with it, I—"

"Oh—I almost forgot my big news!" Lisa interrupted. "Guess who's coming back to town for a visit? Ellen Majors."

Shannon gasped and grabbed for the handlebars of her bike as it started to fall. "Sorry," she said quickly. "The bike just slipped." She suddenly looked very pale.

"Ellen's going to be staying at her aunt's," Lisa added.

No one said anything.

Meg knew they were all thinking the same thoughts, all thinking of a year ago, all thinking of Shannon's brother Evan.

Ellen Majors and Evan had gone together since junior high. Ellen, Meg, and Shannon had been inseparable best friends for even longer.

Then when Evan died, it all fell apart.

Ellen moved away a few months later. No one had heard from her since. Until now.

"It will be great to see her," Meg said brightly, breaking the silence. "It's been so long."

"Yeah," Lisa added, trying to copy Meg's enthusiasm but not quite pulling it off. She and Ellen had never been that close.

Shannon didn't say anything. She was staring at the river, a distant look in her eyes.

"Maybe we should have a party for Ellen," Meg said. She looked at Tony, who looked away.

"Yeah," Lisa repeated.

"Why?" Shannon asked sharply.

"To . . . uh . . . welcome her back," Meg said,

surprised by Shannon's hostility to the idea. "To show her that we still care about her, I guess."

"Evan's still dead," Shannon muttered, not looking at them.

"But we've got to show Ellen that we don't blame her," Meg said, surprised at all the strong feelings she suddenly had. She hadn't realized how much she had missed Ellen all year.

"I guess. . . ." Shannon said unconvincingly, her voice barely audible over the gusting wind.

"I think a party's a great idea," Lisa said, climbing back on her bike. "A surprise party maybe. You know Ellen. She probably wouldn't come if she knew about it in advance. I'll help you two get it together. In fact, I'll start telling everyone about it right away!"

"Count me in," Cory said.

Meg looked back at Tony. He was staring at the ground. "Tony—are you okay?"

"Yeah. Sure."

"Well, what do you think of the party idea?"

"Good. It's okay."

"We've gotta get going," Lisa said, starting up the path. "See you later."

Meg, Shannon, and Tony stood watching them ride off till they disappeared into the trees. "Guess we should be getting back, too," Shannon said. The color still hadn't returned to her face. She looked washed out, drained.

"*I don't believe it!*" Tony screamed.

Both girls were startled. "Tony—what??"

"I've got a flat tire!" He lifted the bike up into the air with both hands.

"Tony, don't—" Meg said.

9

He started to slam the bike to the ground, then thought better of it, and lowered it slowly to the grass.

"Tony, it's just a flat. You can walk it back to—"

"Just go on without me," he muttered. "Go on ahead. See you later."

Seeing that he meant it, the two girls got on their bikes and rode off. When they reached the trees, they could hear him kicking the bike, cursing it loudly.

"What's his problem? Too much raw meat for breakfast?" Shannon asked.

"I don't know," Meg said with a sigh. "Sometimes he just loses it." She wished she did know what his problem was. It wasn't normal to get that angry at a bike—was it?

That night up in her room, Meg was trying to concentrate on her psych paper, but she found her thoughts drifting to Ellen. Ellen with her tall, lanky, blond good looks. She looks so much like Daryl Hannah, everyone always said. Meg wondered if Ellen still looked the same or if she had changed.

A surprise party was a terrific idea. Meg could already see the shocked look on Ellen's face. How happy they all would be again.

The phone rang.

She picked it up, grateful for the interruption.

"Hello, Meg?" A whisper. Like wind blowing into the telephone.

"Who is this?" she asked, a funny feeling forming in the pit of her stomach. "We have a bad connection."

"This is a friend." Still just a whisper.

Who could it be?

"I'm warning you. Don't have a party for Ellen."

"Now, wait a minute—" Meg cried, surprised by her own high-pitched voice, by the fear rising within her. And the anger.

"I'm serious. Dead serious. Don't have a party for Ellen. Don't force me to show you how serious I am."

"Who is this? What kind of a stupid joke—"

She heard a click. The dial tone returned.

She dropped the receiver back onto the phone. The room was silent now. But the whispered voice remained, repeating its threatening message in her ear, the whispers growing louder and louder until she held her ears and forced them to stop.

chapter

2

*M*eg sat at her desk, staring at the phone until it became a white blur. How did she feel?

Scared? No.

Angry? Yes, that was it. Angry and insulted.

Did the caller really think he could frighten her with that stupid, hoarse whispering?

Whoever it was had seen too many bad horror movies, she decided. *Halloween V! Freddy Returns! Friday the 13th, Part 400!* How dumb. Girls in those films were either tramps or frightened idiots. They'd get one scary, whispered phone call and fall to pieces, frightened out of their wits.

Well, this was real life, not a dumb movie. And whoever it was certainly didn't know Meg very well. Maybe she was small and young looking. Maybe she wasn't as sophisticated as a lot of kids at Shadyside. But she wasn't easily pushed around. She had a stubborn streak a mile long. At least that's what her mother always said. And Meg took that as a compliment.

She realized that her heart was pounding. Okay, she admitted to herself, maybe I am a little upset.

She picked up the receiver and pushed Tony's number. The line was busy.

That was annoying. Who could he be talking to?

She wanted to talk to someone. Her parents? No. They'd make too big a deal about it. They'd probably call the police right away, make a big fuss, forbid her to have the party.

And the call was probably just an obnoxious joke some kid from school had decided to play.

She pushed Tony's number again. Still busy.

She hung up and tried Lisa's number. Lisa picked it up after the first ring, and said, "Where are you?"

"Huh?"

"Cory?"

"No. It's Meg."

"Oh. Meg. I'm sorry. I thought it was Cory. He's a little late. Like an hour."

"Sorry," Meg said.

"It's not your fault," Lisa said quickly. She sounded really angry. "I'm trying to look on the bright side. Maybe he was run over by a truck."

"Right. Keep it light." Meg laughed.

"What are you doing? Waiting for Tony?"

"No. We're not going out tonight. I'm supposed to be writing my psych paper."

"But . . ."

"How'd you know there was a *but?*"

"I'm a mind reader," Lisa cracked.

"But I—"

"See? I told you."

"I just got this creepy phone call."

"Really?" Lisa started to sound interested. "Was it a breather? I got a breather once. I couldn't believe it. It was so gross."

"No. This was a whisperer." Meg was beginning to regret telling Lisa about the call. Lisa would only make endless jokes about it. She had such a dry sense of humor. She never took anything seriously.

"What did he whisper?" Lisa asked. "Sweet nothings?"

"No. He told me not to have a party for Ellen."

"He what!?"

"You heard me. He warned me not to have a party."

"Well . . . who do we know who hates parties?"

"I don't know. I couldn't recognize the voice. It was such a strange, hoarse whisper. I really couldn't even tell if it was a boy or a girl."

"I'll bet it was Cory," Lisa said. "He'll do anything to keep from getting over to my house on time."

That was supposed to be funny, but Meg didn't laugh. She felt annoyed that Lisa wasn't taking it more seriously. "It was kinda scary," she told Lisa. "How many kids have you told about Ellen and the party?"

"A lot," Lisa said. "After I ran into you in the park, I went to the mall. I ran into a lot of kids from school. And then I called some kids tonight while I was sitting around waiting for you-know-who. Hey! There's the bell! That's probably him. Gotta run. Later, Meg." She hung up before Meg could say goodbye.

Meg found herself smiling. Lisa complained nonstop about Cory and was constantly putting him down. But when the bell rang, she went running. She really was crazy about him.

Without realizing it, Meg had pushed Tony's number again. This time it rang through. "Hello?"

"Hi, Tony. It's me."

"Oh. Hi." He sounded strange, sort of far away, confused.

"I just got the creepiest phone call. Someone warned me not to have a party for Ellen."

"Me too!" Tony exclaimed.

"What?"

"Yeah. I just got a call. Someone whispering. I think it was a guy. But I couldn't tell. It could have been a girl."

"And what did they say?"

"Not to help out with the party. He said I wouldn't make it to the party if it did take place. I'd be in the hospital."

"Someone's playing a stupid joke—right?"

"I don't know, Meg. Whoever it was sounded pretty serious."

"Oh, come on, Tony. You think he meant it?" Meg was disappointed that Tony was taking this seriously. She wanted him to tell her that it was just a joke, that she should just forget about it. Why did he sound more frightened than she did?

"Who do you think it was, Meg?"

"I don't know. Some kid from school. Someone who's bummed out because he doesn't have a date tonight."

"Maybe." Tony didn't sound convinced. "But we don't know anyone who would do anything that dumb. What if—what if—"

"What, Tony?" Meg asked impatiently.

15

"I don't know. Maybe we should take it seriously. You know, call the police or something."

"What? Get real!" Meg cried angrily. "I wouldn't—"

"I'm just worried about you. That's all," he broke in. "I don't want some creep doing something horrible to you because of a stupid party."

"It isn't a stupid party," Meg insisted. "It's a party for Ellen. My best friend. And I'm not going to let one gross phone call that's probably just some moron's idea of a funny joke stop me from doing what I want to do."

After a long silence Tony agreed. "Yeah. You're right. I guess I just got a little shook."

"Sorry. I didn't mean to yell," Meg said, forcing her voice down, trying to calm herself and speak softly.

"So . . . should I come over and . . . uh . . . comfort you a little?" Tony asked. It sounded more like pleading than asking.

Meg laughed. "No. I shouldn't even be talking to you. I should be writing my psych paper."

"Was that a *yes?*"

"No. It was definitely a *no.*"

"But you mean *yes,* right?"

Meg laughed. It was nice to hear Tony teasing her again, kidding around. "I mean no. Really."

"You mean you need a little comforting, right?"

"No. Give me a break. I need a little writing time. I—"

"You know you won't be able to concentrate on your paper."

"Yes, I will."

"You said yes! I heard you!"

Meg laughed. "I said no."

"But you meant yes?"

"Well . . . maybe."

"Maybe? I'll take a maybe," Tony said happily. "I'll be right over."

"Okay," Meg said, just as happily.

chapter

3

Monday Afternoon

Meg propped her Government text in front of her on the table and looked around the study hall. What was all that noise in the back of the room? She quickly saw that it was just Cory Brooks and his friend David Metcalf from the gymnastics team clowning around on a tabletop.

The study hall was a wide, windowless rectangular room kept blindingly bright by long rows of fluorescent lights suspended high over wooden tables that stretched nearly the width of the room. A small desk stood at the front for the study hall monitor. The desk was empty now, Meg saw. Mrs. Frankel was always late, which gave Cory and David time to do their act on the tabletop.

"Hi," Shannon said, giving Meg a weary wave and taking her usual seat in the row behind her.

"Hi," Meg echoed, searching her bookbag for the invitations she had bought.

"Foster doesn't realize school's almost out," Shan-

18

non complained. "He started a whole new unit this morning."

"Bad break," Meg muttered. She didn't really know what Shannon was talking about. She just knew that Shannon hated Mr. Foster, hated school, and hated work of any kind. Shannon never failed to come into study hall without one complaint or another.

"What do you think of these?" Meg asked, holding up the package of invitations. They were Day-Glo green and pink with the words COME TO A SURPRISE PARTY in silvery ink.

"What are they?" Shannon asked, deftly applying dark red lipstick to her pouty lips.

"Invitations. To Ellen's party. Is that a new color?"

"Yeah. I saw it in a magazine. What do you think?"

"Very . . . uh . . . dramatic."

"Meg, are you sure this party is a good idea?" She dropped the lipstick tube into her bag and rummaged around for a tissue.

"I don't know. I think so. I just think it would be nice to show Ellen we still care. The three of us were best friends for a long time, after all. And Ellen went with Evan for so long, she was practically part of your family."

Meg immediately regretted saying that. Shannon gave her a bitter look. She blotted her lips with the tissue and didn't say anything. Finally, after Meg had turned back to the front, Shannon said, "How can you send out invitations when you don't know where the party will be?"

"I had a great idea about that," Meg said. "You know, my dad's company did the reconstruction on the old Halsey Manor House. He said we could have it for free if we promised to do a perfect cleanup job.''

"That old house in the Fear Street woods?" Shannon cried, surprised. "Yuck. It's creepy back there. Why would you want to—"

"The house has been completely restored. It's like new inside. It's a great place for parties now. And think how nice it'll be not to have any adults around to bug us."

Shannon agreed that the no-adults part was good. But she started to protest about having the party on Fear Street, when Mrs. Frankel showed up and started shouting for everyone to get quiet and start studying.

Meg turned to the front of the room and opened the package of invitations. She started to fill in the first one. All of this talk about Ellen was bringing back a flood of memories. She had a lot of good memories of Ellen. She could remember dozens of exciting and happy times they had spent together since they had met in elementary school.

But now when she thought about Ellen, her mind was drawn to the tragedy of the year before. Ellen and Evan had seemed so much in love. And then, in an instant, Evan was dead. And everything was changed.

Sure, Evan could be crazy sometimes. Sure, he was headstrong and impulsive, always getting himself into one kind of trouble or another. But he could be so lovable, too, so full of fun . . . so full of life.

For a long time it was impossible for any of them to accept the fact that he was dead.

It still was impossible.

Meg looked around the large room. Just about everyone who was involved in the tragic accident, just about everyone who had been involved with Evan, was in this study hall.

Her eyes roamed from face to face. There was Shannon, Evan's sister. She seemed to lose some of *her* life when Evan lost his. She had always been so enthusiastic about everything, so spirited, so ready to have fun. Evan's death had caused her to withdraw. She didn't seem to need her friends as much. It was as if she were pulling into herself, hardening herself, forcing herself not to need anyone else so that she couldn't be hurt by another loss in the same way.

Tony sat near the back, writing intently in a notebook. He and Evan had been buddies. Tony had admired Evan, looked up to him, Meg realized, for his wildness, for the fact that Evan didn't care what people thought of him, for his need to do what he felt like when he felt like it. Tony wished he could be that way. But he was too hung up to be that free and easy, too worried about being poor in a school where most kids were better off, too concerned about being accepted by other kids.

Tony had tried to act tough when he learned that Evan was dead. But at the funeral he broke down and sobbed. Ever since he'd been so moody.

On the other side of the room sat her cousin Brian. With his wavy blond hair, blue eyes, and dimpled grin, Brian looked like an innocent kid. But Meg knew that Brian wasn't as happy-go-lucky as he looked. He was a strange guy who kept mostly to himself.

Right now he wasn't studying. He was reading a copy of *Dragon* magazine. He spent most of his time playing that game *Wizards & Dungeons*, hanging out with his friend Dwayne, talking about Fourth-Level

Warriors and dragons and stuff Meg wasn't the least bit interested in.

Brian and Evan hadn't been friends. But Brian had been in the Fear Street woods that awful day. Brian heard the shot and came running. Brian told everyone that he found Evan lying dead on the ground, Ellen sitting beside him, crying, unable to talk, unable to say a word, unable to explain.

What had Brian been doing alone in the Fear Street woods? No one knew. But Brian had changed, too, because of Evan's death. Afterward, he seemed to become even more involved in the strange fantasy games he played. His grades, which had been excellent, began to slip. His parents, Meg's aunt and uncle, were very worried. But they felt helpless. They didn't know what to do about Brian.

One death, Meg thought. One boy dies in the woods, and so many lives are affected.

She didn't know whom to feel more sorry for. Maybe Ellen. Poor Ellen. Ellen probably felt the most guilty. If only she had been able to stop Evan from going into the Fear Street woods.

The story went that he was going to spend the night there on a dare. Who had dared him? He wouldn't tell Ellen. "I just need some excitement," he told her. He grabbed his father's hunting rifle—just in case—and hurried off to Fear Street. Ellen begged him to leave the rifle home. But he refused.

She went home, but she was too worried to stay there. She went to Fear Street and tried to find him in the woods. She heard a shot, the fatal shot, the shot that changed all of their lives. She heard it and followed the sound of it till she found Evan, lying face down, his left shoe tangled in an upraised tree root.

He was already dead. His foot must have tangled in the root. He must have tripped and fallen, and the gun went off. And that was it.

A few minutes later Brian arrived and found them. Nearly in shock himself, Brian managed to help Ellen out of the woods, away from Fear Street.

A tragic accident. Ellen had never been able to talk about it with anyone. A few months later her family moved away. No one had heard from her—until now.

Maybe we can all be good friends again, Meg thought, with her usual optimism.

"Meg! Meg Dalton! Meg!" A voice broke into her thoughts.

She looked up. Mrs. Frankel was calling her. "Meg, you must be reading a very exciting chapter. I've been calling you for five minutes."

Meg could feel her face growing hot. She knew she was blushing. "Sorry."

"There's a message for you at the office. Come up and get a pass."

Meg left the invitations on the table and, still blushing, went up to get the pass. Who had left her a message? Was it from home? Was someone sick or something?

She grabbed the pass off the desk and started to jog down the hall. "Hi, Meg. What's happening? Did you hear about Gary breaking up with Krista?" It was Lisa sitting in the hall monitor's chair.

"Sorry, Lisa. I'll call you later," Meg said. "I'm kinda in a hurry." Lisa looked surprised that she didn't want to stop for some hot gossip, but Meg kept hurrying on to the office.

When she got inside, out of breath, a nervous feeling in the pit of her stomach, there was no one at the front desk. "Anyone here?" she called. No reply. Finally Miss Markins, the office secretary, appeared from the inner office. She looked surprised to see Meg.

"They told me there was a message here for me," Meg said.

Miss Markins pursed her lips and shook her head. She looked through a stack of pink message slips on her desk. "No. None for you, Meg."

"Are you sure?" Meg insisted. "They just told me in study hall."

Miss Markins looked annoyed that Meg hadn't taken her word, but she grudgingly looked through the messages one more time. "Sorry. Must be a mix-up."

"A mix-up. Yeah. I guess so. Thanks," Meg said. She turned and walked slowly out of the office. In a way she was relieved. A message in the office was seldom good news. But why had someone called her to the office if there was no message there for her?

She stopped and chatted with Lisa for several minutes. There was no point in hurrying back to study hall. She wasn't going to get any studying done. That was obvious. And she could work on the invitations after school.

"What are you doing after school?" she asked Lisa. "Want to come over and help me write invitations?"

"I can't," Lisa said, flipping a pencil up toward the ceiling and catching it. "I have a *Spectator* meeting. We're planning our last issue. I know everyone's waiting breathlessly for it, right?'' Lisa was assistant editor of the school paper.

"But I'd love to help out with the party," Lisa added quickly. "Ellen and I weren't really close or anything, but I always liked her."

They talked for a few more minutes. Then Meg headed back to study hall. Lisa's so funny, Meg thought. She has such a sharp sense of humor. Meg liked Lisa's sophisticated dark looks too. I wish I could be more like her, she thought, instead of such a babyface.

She tossed the hall pass back onto Mrs. Frankel's desk. Mrs. Frankel didn't even look up. Her head was buried in the test papers she was grading. Meg took her seat. She looked around the room for a moment, glanced at her watch, and then looked down at the table.

Oh!

The party invitations.

Someone had cut them all into tiny pieces.

Who would do such a horrible thing?

Meg spun around and faced Shannon. Shannon didn't look up from her book.

"Hey—"

Shannon finally noticed Meg. She closed the book, keeping her place with her finger.

"Did you see anyone come over to my desk?"

"No," Shannon whispered, her eyes on Mrs. Frankel at the front of the room. "I wasn't here. I went to the library to get this book. I just got back a second ago."

Meg stared hard at Shannon. She felt guilty for

suspecting her friend. Shannon wasn't happy about having the party for Ellen, but she would never do something like this—would she?

She started to show Shannon the cut-up invitations, then she thought about the whispered phone call she had gotten on Saturday night.

Was the creep who made that call right in the same study hall with her now? Was it Shannon?

No. Of course not. How stupid.

But then, who was it?

She gathered up the pieces of the invitations and began to sweep them into her bag. Then she searched in her bag for a pen. There was ten minutes left to study hall. She could start making a list of all the things she needed to buy for the party.

Someone yawned loudly near the back door, and everyone laughed. Meg found a pen and opened her trapper-keeper to a clean sheet of notebook paper. *Things to Buy,* she wrote up at the top.

"Meg, please come up here," Mrs. Frankel called.

Now what?

She closed the trapper-keeper and hurried up to Mrs. Frankel's desk. "You seem to have another message at the office," Mrs. Frankel said, looking perturbed.

"Are you sure?" Meg asked.

"I'm not sure about anything around here," Mrs. Frankel said dryly. "But you'd better go check."

Meg hurried back down the hall, passing Lisa with a shrug, as if to say, I don't know what I'm doing back here again, either.

Maybe Miss Markins found the first message, Meg thought. And yes, when she got to the office, Miss

Markins had a long, white envelope for her. "I guess someone left this for you," Miss Markins said. "I just found it on the counter. I didn't see who left it."

Meg thanked her and took the envelope out into the hall to open. It was sealed tightly and took her a while to tear open. She put out a piece of lined, white notebook paper and unfolded it.

The words on the paper were written in sloppy block letters with a red crayon. She read them three times.

MEG, I'M WATCHING YOU. DON'T HAVE THE PARTY. I DON'T WANT TO HURT YOU—BUT I WILL.

chapter
4

Later, Monday Afternoon

"*H*ey, Shannon—wait up! I want to talk to you!"

Shannon turned around in the crowded hallway, swinging her bulging backpack over her shoulder. "Can't. I'm late. I have a dentist appointment."

Meg pushed through a laughing group of kids and hurried to catch up to her. The bell had rung before Meg could get back to the study hall. She looked for Tony. She wanted to show him the threatening note. But she didn't see him in the room or in the hall.

"Shannon—wait up!"

"I can't. Really. Call me tonight, okay?" Shannon turned and disappeared around the corner.

"Hey—you see Shannon?" It was Dwayne Colligan. He towered over Meg. All she could see was his blue T-shirt stretched tightly across his muscular chest.

He's so big, he doesn't look like a teenager, Meg thought. Maybe he was held back five or six times. All of the hours he should have been studying and doing homework, he must have been working out.

"You just missed her," she said coldly. She didn't like Dwayne, and she didn't like the idea of Dwayne and Shannon. He wasn't good enough for her. He wasn't good enough for her dog. She was glad that Shannon agreed. Meg didn't even like Dwayne hanging out with her cousin Brian, but there was nothing she could do about that.

"If you see her, tell her I've got something for her!" Dwayne shouted over the noise of the corridor.

"What?" Meg asked.

He gave her an exaggerated wink and a big, dirty smile in reply, and trotted off, laughing as if he'd just made the best joke in the world.

Ugh, Meg thought. He's so gross. Shannon is going to have to tell him to get lost, once and for all.

She walked back to the study hall to collect her things, then headed up to her locker on the second floor. "Hey, Tony—hi!" He was standing at his locker, leaning against the wall with one hand, reading a piece of paper in his other hand.

When he looked up, she saw that his face was troubled. "Oh, hi, Meg." He looked back down at the paper.

She dropped her backpack on the floor and grabbed the paper out of his hand. It was another note with big block letters scrawled in red crayon. "You got one too?" As she read his, she bent down and pulled hers out of the bookbag to show him.

His read: TONY—DON'T LET THE PARTY TAKE PLACE—OR YOU'RE DEAD MEAT. A FRIEND.

"I found it in my locker," Tony said, reading her

note quickly and handing it back to her. He seemed quite shaken. "Who could have done it? It's someone who knows us both, who knows where our lockers are, who knows where we are."

"I don't know," Meg said, shaking her head, re-reading his note. "I haven't a clue."

"Still think it's just a joke?" he asked. He took the note from her hands and crumpled it up into a ball.

"No. I guess not. But who would want to stop this party? Why would someone be so desperate to stop it that they'd do *this?*"

Tony shrugged. He took a maroon sweatshirt from his locker and pulled it over his head. "We don't know how desperate they really are," he said, straightening his hair with both hands.

"What do you mean?"

"I mean, how far will they go to stop us? Will they really hurt us?"

She stared into Tony's eyes and caught the fear inside. "That's ridiculous," she said softly. But now she wasn't so sure. She hadn't been at all frightened. She only felt anger that someone would be pulling something like this. But seeing the fear on Tony's face made her a little afraid, too.

"I really don't want to find out how desperate they are," he said, looking away to evade her staring eyes.

"What do you mean?"

"I think we should forget about the party. We can see Ellen and have a good time without throwing a big surprise party with a hundred kids—can't we?"

"That's not the point," Meg said sharply. "We can't let this creep—whoever it is—push us around. If we want to throw a party, we're going to throw a party. It's a free country, right?"

"But someone really doesn't want us to throw that party," Tony said. He picked up the balled-up note and started tossing it from hand to hand.

"I don't care," Meg said. "I don't care!" She could feel her anger rising. "We're having that party. And we're going to find out who's trying to frighten us— and get them to stop!"

"Meg, please—" He grabbed her shoulder, hard at first, then loosened his grip. "Think about this. Think about it carefully. We both should think about it before we decide what to do."

"No. I've already decided," she said stubbornly. She pulled away from him. She realized that she was annoyed that Tony would give in, would back down so easily. Was he frightened for her, or for himself? she wondered.

He was just frightened.

She had another thought. What about Shannon? Had Shannon received any threatening phone calls or notes?

No.

She surely would have mentioned them.

Shannon was as much behind the party as Meg and Tony, wasn't she? Why wasn't she being threatened too?

"Someone cut up my invitations," she told Tony.

"Huh?"

"I had them in study hall. I was called to the office, and when I got back they'd been cut into tiny pieces."

"Wasn't Shannon sitting right behind you?"

"Yes. But she said she went out. To the library. She didn't see who did it."

"Funny," he said, thinking hard. "I didn't see her leave the room."

"You didn't?"

"No. I was there the whole time. I'm sure she was too."

"Well, that's weird." She leaned back against the lockers. "Tony, you don't think Shannon—"

"I don't know. She didn't really want the party at first, did she? But I don't think she'd—"

"No. Of course not. She's my best friend."

She picked up her note and read it again. Did the big block letters look as if they could have been made by a girl? Hmm . . . maybe. It was hard to say.

Meg felt a chill slide down her spine. She suddenly had the feeling that she and Tony were being watched. She looked up from the note.

Yes. Someone was staring at them from across the hall.

It was her cousin Brian. And he had the eeriest look on his face. How long had he been watching them? Why was he just standing there, staring like that?

"Brian?" she called.

He looked startled, as if he hadn't planned on being seen.

Tony took a few steps toward him.

Brian turned and ran.

chapter

5

Monday Night

"*M*eg, what are you doing up there?"

"Homework, Mom!" Meg shouted. "If I don't finish this psych paper, I'll get an Incomplete in the course."

"I thought you finished that paper days ago," Mrs. Dalton called up the stairs.

"No. I . . . uh . . . I've been working on it. But some other things came up."

"Well, get to work, then."

"Mom, thanks a bunch for the advice. You know, if I have to spend the whole night discussing it with you, I won't get too far."

"Well, aren't you the tense one these days! So touchy!"

"Mom, please—give me a break."

Silence.

She heard her mother walk away from the stairs.

Meg looked down at the sheet of notebook paper in front of her on the desk. She wasn't working on her psych paper. Instead she had written on the top line: LIST OF SUSPECTS.

33

She started to write the number *1*, but her pencil lead broke. She tossed the pencil across the room and picked up another. Then she wrote the number *1*, and beside it the name *Brian*.

Then under *Brian* she wrote: "Why?"

A) Because he was staring at Tony and me so strangely.
B) Because he ran away when he saw that we saw him.
C) ?

She sucked on the pencil eraser. Why? Why? Why? What reason could Brian possibly have for wanting to stop Ellen's party?

She searched her memory for a clue. Brian and Ellen. Brian and Ellen . . . Nothing. Zero. Zip. She couldn't come up with anything.

Brian and Ellen were only acquaintances, never even friends, really. Brian certainly had no reason to hate Ellen or even dislike her.

Brian had been the one to help Ellen, to rescue her, that day a year ago, that day in the Fear Street woods when Evan shot himself and Brian found Ellen there, crying, dazed . . .

Evan.

Ellen and Evan.

Did Evan's death have something to do with this?

Meg removed the pencil from her mouth and wrote: NOTE: DOES SOMEONE HATE ELLEN BECAUSE OF EVAN?

Then she added a second name to her list of suspects: *Shannon*.

And under *Shannon* she wrote: "Why?"

A) Because Evan was her brother. Maybe she blames Ellen for what happened.
B) Shannon was in study hall when the invitations were torn up.
C) Shannon wasn't enthusiastic about the party from the start.
D) Shannon's been different since Evan died.

She crossed out *D*, drawing heavy black lines through it. It wasn't fair, Meg decided. They had *all* been different since Evan died.

Shannon is my best friend, Meg thought, tapping the pencil rapidly on the desktop. She wouldn't try to scare me, would she? She wouldn't try such stupid horror-movie tricks.

Would she?

Would Shannon be honest with her about the party, about Ellen?

"I don't know," Meg said, not realizing she was speaking aloud. Shannon, she decided, would have to stay on the list of suspects.

And who else?

"Meg—how's the paper coming along?"

Oh, no. Her mother was back already!

"Fine, Mom—till you interrupted!" she shouted. "You made me lose my train of thought."

"Maybe that's because you think with your *ca-boose!*" Her mother laughed hysterically. She always loved her own rotten jokes.

"Thanks for the support, Mom!"

She heard her Mom walk away again, still chuckling.

Her eyes returned to the sheet of paper. She was surprised to see that without realizing it, she had written a name after the number *3: Ellen.*

Why was Ellen a suspect?

A) Because someone from school could have called her and told her about the party.
B) Because Ellen never liked parties.
C) She never called or wrote to any of her old friends. Maybe she doesn't want to see everyone.
D) She never even explained why her family moved away from Shadyside so suddenly.

Yes, Ellen had to be considered a suspect, Meg realized. But how would she have gotten the red-crayoned notes to Meg and Tony?

A friend. Someone in school could be helping her.

So maybe there were *two* people Meg should be looking for.

She wrote the number *4.* Is there a fourth suspect? Is there someone else who knew about the party, knew Meg and Tony had a good reason to stop the party?

She couldn't think of anyone. So she wrote down *Dwayne.*

Why?

"Because I don't like him."

The phone rang.

She stared at it, reluctant to pick it up. Maybe I'll just let it ring, she thought.

But she knew she couldn't do that. If a phone rang, she always had to pick it up, even if it wasn't hers. She couldn't bear to let a phone call go unanswered.

She let it ring one more time, took a deep breath, and picked it up. "Hello?"

"Hi, Meg."

"Tony?"

"You're safe? You're okay?"

"Tony—what do you mean? You sound terrible!"

"I—I was worried about you. I . . . well . . . I think someone was following me tonight."

"Following you? Where?"

"Following me home. I was at my dad's gas station, see, helping out. He had the car, so I walked home. It was weird. I kept seeing these shadows. But every time I turned around, there was no one there."

"And?"

"And then there were footsteps behind me. So I started running. And the footsteps started running too."

"Did you see who it was? Was it a boy or a girl?"

"I never saw. It was pitch black. And whoever it was stayed pretty far back."

"Are you sure there really was someone there?"

"Of course I'm sure," he snapped angrily. "I'm not totally nuts, you know."

"Sorry, Tony. Don't shout at me. Please. I just wanted to know—"

"Listen, this is getting scary, Meg. I think this person really means business."

"Didn't you get a look at whoever it was at all? Didn't you see anything?"

"No."

"Was he tall or short?"

"I don't know. I just ran. I just wanted to get home. *Give me a break—okay?*"

"Sorry. Please don't yell."

"I called you right away. I thought maybe they tried something—maybe they followed you, too, or something."

"No. I'm fine. Really."

"This party, Meg. I don't know."

"What do you mean?"

"I mean, is it worth it? It's just a stupid party."

"Yes, but now it's a principle," Meg said.

"A principle? Aw, come on—forget about principles. Somebody followed me, Meg. I'm really scared. I'm not willing to risk my life for a party—"

"But don't you see?" she cried impatiently. "It isn't just a party. If somebody wants to stop it so badly, there's got to be more to it. There's something else going on here, Tony. And we've got to find out what it is."

"You're really enjoying this, aren't you," he said with some bitterness. "You're a real Nancy Drew, huh? You like being Miss Detective. You think this is exciting."

"Kind of," Meg admitted. "But I also don't like being pushed around by someone who thinks they can tell me—"

"Count me out," Tony interrupted.

"What?"

"Count me out. You heard me."

"Out of what?"

"Out of everything. Out of the party. Out of . . . you and me."

The words seemed to sting her ears. The sting traveled quickly to her chest. It was so . . . unexpected.

"You mean that?"

"Good-bye," he said quietly and hung up the phone.

Meg slammed the receiver down angrily. Of course, Tony was just mouthing off without thinking again, she told herself. Of course he really doesn't mean it. He doesn't really want to break up with me over this.

Or does he?

He did sound really frightened. Meg asked herself if she was frightened too. No, she decided. She wasn't at all scared. She was too furious to be scared. She wasn't going to give up the party. And she wasn't going to give up Tony.

"I'll find out who's doing this and I'll find out why," she said aloud.

She picked up the receiver and started to push Tony's number. But then she thought better of it. "I'll give him a day or two to calm down. Then I'll apologize."

She wasn't going to allow herself to believe that he really had broken up with her. She wasn't going to believe it. No way. She realized she was biting her lower lip and now it was bleeding.

How was she to concentrate on her psych paper? She couldn't. She'd have to try again tomorrow. But what should she do now?

She looked down at her list of suspects. Number 3: *Ellen*.

She didn't want Ellen to be on the list. The party was for Ellen, after all. All of this trouble was for Ellen. It really would be easier if she could cross Ellen off the list.

I'll call her.

The idea seemed to float into her mind from out of nowhere. Such a good idea.

I'll call her and tell her how happy I am that she's coming for a visit.

She felt her throat tighten. A feeling of dread started up from her stomach. No. It won't be hard. It won't be hard to talk to Ellen. We were best friends, after all.

She picked up the phone and pushed Information. She realized her hands were suddenly ice cold. It didn't take long to get Ellen's phone number.

I should have called her sooner, she scolded herself. Why did I wait all these months for Ellen to call me?

She pushed the upstate area code and the number. It rang once, twice, the dull rings sounding very far away. Ellen picked up after the third ring. "Hello?"

"Ellen? It's me. Meg."

"Meg? I don't believe it! Hi!" Ellen shrieked. She sounded thrilled to hear from Meg. Meg let out a sigh of relief. She felt much better.

"So how are you?"

"Fine. Just fine. How are *you?*"

"Okay. Not bad," Meg said. "It's funny to hear your voice. It's been so long."

"I know," Ellen said, sounding guilty. "I've been meaning to write or something. I just got so busy and—"

"How's your new school?"

"Okay, I guess. It's different, really different from Shadyside. I'll tell you about it when I see you. I'm coming down, you know."

"Yeah. That's why I'm calling. I wanted to tell you how glad I am. I—"

"I'll be staying at my Aunt Amy's. I hope we'll have lots of time to spend together."

"Me too, Ellen. I really miss you." Meg blurted that out. She hadn't really meant to sound so emotional. It just came out. It felt so good to be talking to her old friend, so comfortable, as if things hadn't changed at all.

"Me too."

"You want to do anything special, or see anyone, or anything?" Meg asked, talking rapidly, excitedly.

"No, not really. How's Tony?"

"He's okay. The same, I guess."

"You two still together?"

"Yeah." Up until two minutes ago. But why go into that?

"I'm so happy you called, Meg. I can't wait to see you."

"Me too."

They chattered on for a few more minutes, not really talking about anything. Then Meg decided she'd better say good-bye before the call got expensive enough for her father to complain about. Ellen promised to call as soon as she got to Shadyside, and then they hung up.

Meg felt really good. What a nice talk! Ellen sounded the same as ever. And she'd been so happy that Meg had called.

Meg picked up the pencil and started to cross out Ellen's name from her suspect list. But then she stopped. She stared at the paper, thinking hard.

Ellen had seemed so happy, so thrilled, so enthusiastic.

41

Too enthusiastic.

Too happy.

That wasn't like Ellen at all.

It was all so forced, so phony. She was being super-cheery, dripping with sweetness, Meg realized.

She wasn't being Ellen. She wasn't being herself. What was she trying to hide?

chapter

6

"Why don't you hit him?"

"I tried that. He thought it was funny."

"And I guess reasoning with him is out."

Lisa rolled her dark eyes and sighed. "That's all I do is reason with him. Cory and I spend all our time together reasoning with each other. That's one of the main reasons we don't have any fun. We're too busy reasoning with each other and discussing why we're not getting along. We don't have any time left to *get* along!"

Meg tilted the can to her lips and took a long drink of Diet Coke. She slumped down low in the big leather couch, holding the can in her lap. "I like this room," she said after a long silence, looking around at the dark wood-paneled walls, the bookshelves up to the ceiling with the big-screen TV built in to the center, the glass doors that opened onto a backyard terrace. "We don't have a den."

"You're not trying to change the subject or anything, are you?" Lisa asked with a wry grin.

Meg smiled. "I just don't know what to say. Tony and I aren't getting along, either. We had a big fight about the party for Ellen. He's really frightened that whoever's been trying to scare us really means business. But I told him I wasn't going to let some creep frighten me out of what I want to do."

"Maybe you *are* being stubborn about it, Meg. Maybe Tony is right," Lisa said, pulling her long legs over the side of the leather armchair she was sitting in. "At least, Tony's worried about you. If someone was threatening me, Cory would probably say, 'Yeah, but what's on TV tonight?' "

Meg laughed. Lisa did a great Cory impression. "Maybe you should just lighten up on Cory for a while," she said. "He's really a good guy. Maybe you're just expecting too much from him. You two have grown up together. He lives right next door. It's natural he'd take you a *little* for granted. In a way, he should."

Lisa finished off her Diet Coke and crushed the can in her hand. "What's with you, Meg? I didn't want any good advice. I just wanted to complain."

Both girls laughed.

"But I'm being selfish," Lisa said, tossing the crushed soda can toward a wastebasket by the desk across the room. "Hey—two points!" Her face turned serious. "You came over here to tell me about the terrible things that have been happening to you, and all I do is talk about Cory and me. I'm sorry. You've got real problems. You know, maybe you should call the police."

"Sure, Lisa," Meg said, pulling herself up with some difficulty. The couch was so soft, she had sunk down into the cushion. "I'll go to the police and tell them that someone cut up my party invitations in study hall. That'll really get 'em excited, right. They'll probably get the whole police squad out on that case! Maybe a S.W.A.T. team too!"

"How do you get your skin like that?" Lisa asked.

"What?"

"Your skin. It's so perfect. Like a baby's skin."

"Huh? Lisa—" Meg's hand went up involuntarily to her face.

"Your face always looks like you just washed it. Fresh-scrubbed. That's what they call it. You have that fresh-scrubbed look."

"I guess now it's *you* who wants to change the subject," Meg grumbled.

"No. Sorry. I just got distracted." Lisa stood up and stretched. Then she walked to the glass doors and looked out. "Look, Meg, maybe you should just forget about the surprise party. Then all of your problems will go away."

"But I don't want to," Meg told her, not meaning to sound so whiny. "I really care about Ellen. I really want to show her that we still care about her. And . . ."

"And?"

"And I'm really curious now. I want to find out why someone is so desperate to stop this party."

"What do you mean?"

"It isn't just a silly prank. Someone has a serious reason for trying to stop the party. But what could it be?"

"Is it because someone really hates Ellen?"

45

"I don't know of anyone who hated Ellen. Do you?" Meg asked.

Lisa stared out into the darkness. "No. But then, what else could it be? Maybe it has something to do with Evan."

"Evan. Yeah. I was thinking that too. What made you say Evan, Lisa?"

"I don't know. When I think of Ellen, I guess I automatically think of Evan. You know. Ellen and Evan. We always talked about them together. But Evan has been dead for a year. What could he possibly have to do with someone trying to stop the party?"

"I don't know. It's a total mystery. But it's a mystery I want to solve. That's why I'm not going to give up about this party. I'm not going to quit. If I give up now, we'll never know what this is all about."

"Did anyone ever tell you you're a very stubborn person?"

"Everyone," Meg said. "What are you looking at?"

"Just looking across the backyard. There's a light on in Cory's room. I wonder if he's up there." She stared out a while longer, then backed away from the glass doors and dropped back onto the black leather armchair. "So do you have any idea at all who might be trying to frighten you and Tony? Any hunches?"

"Promise you won't laugh," Meg said cautiously.

"You know me," Lisa replied.

"Yes, I do. That's why I said 'promise you won't laugh.' "

"Okay. I promise. But my fingers may be crossed a little."

"Well, I made a list of suspects."

"And?"

"Well, number one on the list is Brian."

Lisa sat up straight. "Brian? Why Brian? He's your cousin, isn't he?"

"Yeah. Second cousin. But that doesn't rule him out. He may be in my family, but he's still as weird as they come. Always hanging around with Dwayne, playing those fantasy games."

"I don't know," Lisa said doubtfully. "Who else is on your list?"

"Shannon."

"What?!" Lisa's dark eyes lit up with surprise.

"Shannon sits right behind me in study hall. She could easily have cut up the invitations. When I asked her about it, she said she didn't see anything because she went to the library. But Tony was in the study hall too. He says he never saw Shannon leave the room."

"And what about the phone call and the note?"

"She could have been the one," Meg said, sounding less sure of herself.

"But, Meg, she's your best friend, right?"

"Right. I know it's a crazy idea, Lisa. But Shannon hasn't been the same since Evan died. And she seemed to be very much against this party right from the beginning."

Lisa sighed and shook her head. "Your cousin and your best friend. Who else is on the list—your mom and dad?"

"Come on, Lisa. I—"

"Not very likely suspects, Meg. Why would Shannon try to scare you like that? Why wouldn't she just tell you that—"

"I don't know. I just get weird vibes from her, that's all. Maybe she blames Ellen for what happened to

Evan. Maybe she's afraid of something that might happen at the party. I don't really know. I just—"

"Well, go ask her, then."

"What?"

"You heard me," Lisa said, jumping to her feet and starting to pace back and forth. "She's your best friend. You don't want to be walking around with your best friend on your list of suspects. So just go ask Shannon if she's the one. Ask her why she doesn't want a party for Ellen. Talk to her. Straight. That's what friends are for, right?"

"Uh . . . I think maybe I'm like you," Meg said, straightening her sweatshirt. "I didn't want any good advice. I just wanted to complain."

Meg thanked Lisa for the talk and headed out to the car. The cool air revived her, cleared her head. Maybe Lisa is right, she thought. Maybe I will have a little talk with Shannon tomorrow. She slid into her mother's little Toyota and headed for home, rehearsing over and over what she would say.

She pulled up the drive and stopped a few inches from the garage. A light over the garage door cast a dim yellow glow onto the shingles of the house.

Meg started to climb out of the car, then, startled, inhaled sharply. That shadow on the porch—it wasn't usually there, was it?

Was someone waiting for her in the darkness?

chapter
7

*M*eg slumped down in the seat, staring hard at the shadow on the porch shingles. The shadow didn't move.

Her finger was on the ignition key. Her first impulse was to start the car up again, back down the drive, and race away.

But maybe it was Tony waiting for her there. How many times had he done that—waited for her on the doorstep without ringing the bell and going in? Dozens!

Maybe he had come to apologize, to make up.

She pulled the key from the ignition and started to open the door.

Or maybe it wasn't Tony.

Maybe it was the creep who had called her. Maybe it was the creep who had followed Tony.

The shadow didn't move.

How was it possible for a person to stand so still?

She pushed open the car door a few inches. "Who's there?" she called, surprised that she sounded more angry than afraid.

Silence.

"Who is it? Is someone there?"

Silence. The shadow didn't move.

"Tony—is that you?"

It wasn't possible for someone to stay that still for so long.

She climbed out of the car and crept silently across the wet lawn toward the porch. She could feel the fear rise and catch in her throat.

She took another step, another step, her sneakers making soft, squishy sounds in the tall, dew-covered grass. Why am I doing this? she asked herself. Why aren't I running away? Why am I being so stupid?

She stopped at the side of the porch. "Who's there?"

And then she laughed.

The shadow was made by a stack of tall flower pots her father had left on the fence railing.

"Meg, you're losing it," she said aloud, and breathed a heavy sigh.

She hurried inside to get some sleep, locking the door securely behind her.

Thursday Afternoon

Meg poked her fork at the bright orange substance on her plate. If it was macaroni and cheese, where was the macaroni? If it was just cheese, why was it such a weird color?

The lunchroom wasn't very crowded for some reason. Maybe other kids had heard they were serving this orange sticky stuff today and hurried somewhere else for lunch. Cory Brooks and some of his pals from the gymnastics team were clowning around at a table near the door. "Don't they ever get tired of throwing milk cartons at each other?" Meg asked herself.

The windows along the far wall were open, since it was the warmest spring day yet. The brassy bleats from the band out on the practice field, playing "Pomp and Circumstance" over and over again as they prepared for the seniors' graduation, were annoying everyone.

Meg straightened the sleeves of her white blouse. She took a tentative bite of the macaroni and cheese substance. It had no taste whatsoever.

She looked up to see Shannon carrying a tray toward her table. Shannon made a sour face. She was inhaling the aroma of the food substance on her plate.

Oh boy, Meg thought, taking a deep breath. She knew that confronting Shannon wasn't going to be easy. But now was as good a time as any. She might as well get it over with.

"What *is* this stuff?" Shannon asked, dropping her tray in front of Meg's and pulling out a chair with a loud scraping noise.

"It's just Styrofoam," Meg said. "Like those crunchy things they put in packages when they ship them somewhere."

Shannon poked it with a fork, just the way Meg had. "Hey—I think it tried to bite my fork!"

Meg didn't laugh. She looked Shannon in the eye

and stared hard as if searching for an answer to the question she hadn't asked yet.

"What's wrong with you?" Shannon asked, dropping her fork onto the tray. "You're weirder than usual today."

"I . . . I have to ask you a question," Meg said softly.

"Go ahead. Ask. But get that morbid look off your face."

"Sorry." Meg didn't realize she looked so grim. She wanted to toss this off as a light, silly thing. But now that was impossible. "Look. I know this is ridiculous, but I just have to ask."

"Go ahead," Shannon pleaded. "The suspense is killing me."

Meg took a deep breath. She could feel her face growing red. "Did you call me late at night and send me a threatening note?"

"What?"

"Did you? I got this call and a note, and—"

"About what?" Shannon looked genuinely confused.

"Threatening me. Telling me not to have the party for Ellen."

"Threatening you? You think I was threatening you?"

Meg realized she had made a mistake. "No, I . . ." She struggled to think of something to say to get herself out of this.

"Meg—what exactly are you accusing me of?" Shannon's voice rose several octaves. Her hands gripped the edge of the table.

"I wasn't accusing you. I was just asking," Meg

said lamely. "I just wanted you to tell me it wasn't you. That's all."

"Well, it wasn't me," Shannon sneered. Her surprise was quickly turning to anger. "Why on earth would I threaten you, Meg?"

"I don't know," Meg said. "Someone's been making horrible threats. Someone followed Tony and . . . I . . . I'm upset, Shannon. I guess I'm not thinking clearly. I—"

"I guess you're not," Shannon said coldly.

"But, Shannon, I didn't mean—"

"I think you did what you meant to do. I don't understand why you wanted to insult me, why you'd accuse me. I always thought we were good friends. I always thought we trusted each other. I'd never accuse *you* of anything like that. But I guess we're different. Very different. More different than I thought." She choked out the last words. She seemed about to lose control.

"Shannon, you're taking this the wrong way. I only meant—"

Shannon, her face knotted up in anger, pushed away from the table, turned, and walked with long, quick strides out of the lunchroom.

Meg sat frozen, staring after her, feeling like a real rat.

Thank you, Lisa, for such good advice, she thought. Now I have no friends at all. No Tony. No Shannon.

She realized she couldn't blame Lisa for what had happened. She never should have done it. She never should have confronted Shannon that way. She never should have accused her.

But wait.

Wasn't Shannon overreacting a bit? Why did Shannon get so hysterical so quickly? She usually didn't have such a short fuse. Was she trying to hide the fact that it *was* she who was terrorizing Meg? Was she carrying on like that to keep Meg from questioning her, from finding out the truth?

No. Meg knew Shannon. Shannon's shock and anger were real. She wasn't putting it on.

And she had every right to be shocked and angry.

Meg had been a fool. And a cruel one at that. Now Shannon would probably never speak to her again. And why should she?

Meg sat miserably staring at the door to the lunchroom, trying to will Shannon back in so that she could apologize, so that she could explain.

And where was Tony? Why was he being so stubborn? Didn't he know that she needed him now?

After a while she realized she was starving. She shoved the tray of yellow macaroni to the side and lifted the brown paper bag from her lap. She always bought lunch and brought a lunch too. The lunchroom food was just never enough.

She started to unwrap the bag.

That's funny, she thought. There's something leaking in here.

Leaking? How could it be leaking? She had only packed a sandwich and an apple. It must be—"

She reached her hand in. She felt something wet and sticky. And thick.

"OH!"

She pulled her hand out fast, tipping over the bag. A dark red liquid oozed out, spilling down her white blouse, onto her skirt. Meg pulled up her hand. It was covered with the warm liquid. It dripped down her wrist and onto her arm and puddled on the lunch tray.

"It's blood!" she cried. "My lunch bag is filled with *blood!*"

chapter

8

Thursday Night

*M*eg couldn't concentrate on her psych paper. She stared down at her desk without seeing it. All she could see was the sticky, dripping lunch bag, which had turned out to be filled with red paint. Then Shannon's face. Then the dripping blood. Then Shannon's face again, the hurt look, the look of complete shock, of betrayal.

"I've got to apologize," she said aloud. She couldn't bear to have Shannon so mad at her. She couldn't bear to feel so guilty, so . . . wrong.

The car was parked in front of the house, but Meg felt like walking. Walking the nine or ten blocks would give her time to think of what she was going to say.

It had rained most of the afternoon, and the air still smelled fresh and wet. Small puddles of water on the pavement reflected shimmering yellow light from the streetlamps. Meg jumped over the bigger puddles, walking quickly.

She reached Shannon's house without deciding exactly what to say. She just wanted to throw herself on Shannon's mercy and beg her forgiveness. Shannon could be cold and hard, she knew. Especially this past year. It might take a lot of begging. But what choice did she have?

The Harper's house was set back high over a sweeping lawn of carefully trimmed grass, a large, old weeping willow looming over the drive like an ancient servant guarding the entranceway. The front of the house was completely dark, but Meg knew that the family always stayed in the family room and kitchen in the back.

Shannon opened the door a few seconds after Meg rang the bell. Her face fell. "Oh. It's you."

"I came to grovel at your feet," Meg said, trying unsuccessfully to keep her voice steady. "I just want to apologize. I'll do anything. Really. I feel terrible."

"That's good," Shannon said, looking past Meg.

"You've got to accept my apology," Meg said. "You're my best friend and—"

"Come in," Shannon said, pulling back the door. Her voice was flat and unfriendly.

Meg followed her into the entranceway. Shannon was wearing tan Bermuda shorts and a sleeveless white undershirt-type top. Her arms and legs looked very pale, almost ivory-pale. Everyone looked really pale in May, Meg decided, after the long winter.

Shannon led her into the dark living room, switched on a brass floor lamp, and took a seat on a narrow red velvet antique loveseat.

Meg hated Shannon's living room. Partly because the furniture was so fancy and so uncomfortable. And partly because of the large photograph of Evan that hung in a dark wooden frame in the center of the front wall. It was impossible to stand or sit in the room without staring at the photograph, and it made Meg even more uncomfortable than the hard, ornate chairs.

It wasn't at all a typical photo of Evan. For one thing, he was wearing a dark sports jacket and a tie. He had just come from some sort of family function, a wedding maybe. His blond hair, usually wild and unruly, was slicked back, his eyes were set in a blank stare, and he was wearing a forced smile that Meg had never seen on him in real life.

Meg figured this was the way Mr. and Mrs. Harper wanted to remember Evan—not the way he was, a troublemaker, a wild man, but the way he looked in this picture, civilized and completely in control.

Staring at the photograph always brought back memories of the other side of Evan for Meg, though. It was as if her mind were rejecting this false image, this smooth stranger, to bring back the real boy she knew with all of his faults and all of his problems.

She suddenly remembered a night downstairs in the game room in Shannon's basement. Who was there that night? All of them—Shannon and Ellen and Meg and Tony and Evan. Tony and Evan were shooting pool on the large table in the center of the room. The girls were trying to play doubles Ping-Pong with only three people.

Meg could hear the sounds in that room again, the shouts, the loud laughter, the pop of the Ping-Pong ball against the paddles, the clicking sound the ball made as the girls chased it across the tile floor, and the solid tap of the pool cues hitting the shiny, colored billiard balls.

Evan was in a particularly wild mood that night. He had accidentally rammed one of the family's cars into the back of a pickup truck that afternoon, and Tony was laughing at him. "It wasn't my fault, man," Evan declared, knocking the three-ball into a corner pocket and grinning at Tony, pleased with himself.

"You plow into the back of a truck, and it isn't your fault?" Tony scoffed.

"No way. That truck was going below the minimum speed on the thruway. So I couldn't help it. He was going too slow!"

Tony laughed and missed his shot.

"So you tried to speed him up by giving him a little bump," Ellen muttered.

"A little bump that totaled your car!" Tony fell on the floor laughing, holding his sides.

"So you're both against me, huh?" Evan said, staring at Ellen. Suddenly he wasn't joking anymore.

"No, Evan. Tony and I—"

"I saw you!" Evan cried, swatting his pool cue hard against the side of the table. "You think it's a big joke, huh? Some idiot truck driver slows down and forces me to crash, and you two think it's a riot!"

"Come on, man—" Tony started, holding up his hands as if in surrender.

"No. *You* come on!" Evan cried. He raised his pool cue like a sword and started swinging it against Tony's cue. *Click-click-CLICK*. Evan, his eyes wild, his blond hair tossed back, started hitting Tony's cue harder and harder, challenging Tony to fence with him.

"Evan—stop!" Ellen cried.

He swung his cue like a baseball bat, meaning to hit Tony. But Tony ducked and the cue hit Ellen on the shoulder. It made a loud, sharp sound. She cried out and backed against the basement wall. "Evan!"

But Evan ignored her. He and Tony were standing on the pool table now, going at each other with grim determination, like a movie swordfight. Meg remembered the look on Tony's face. It was all just a goof to him. He was having a great time.

But Evan looked serious, intent on winning. It soon became obvious to everyone but Tony that Evan was really fighting. The pool cues clattered against each other. Both boys leaped down from the pool table and moved across the floor, attacking and thrusting.

Evan's face grew bright red. He was scowling, and his eyes seemed to be clamped shut. Suddenly he swung down hard. There was a loud crack.

Tony's eyes went wide, then rolled up in his head. He slumped down to the floor. Blood began to pour down his hair from the top of his head.

Evan didn't look down at Tony. He was studying his pool cue. "I think I cracked it," he said, very concerned.

Ellen began to shriek at him. "How could you do that to Tony?"

Meg remembered the surprised look on Evan's face. He didn't seem to realize what he had done. He looked down. His expression changed, his features all seeming to drop at once. He bent over Tony. "Hey—you okay? That was an accident. I guess my arm slipped."

"That's okay," Tony said groggily. He smiled up at his friend. He would always forgive Evan for anything.

Meg and Shannon decided to drive Tony to the Emergency Room at Shadyside Hospital. As they left, they could still hear Ellen down in the basement, yelling at Evan, trying to make him admit that it wasn't an accident. Tony got five stitches.

It was a horrible night. But no one ever knew what to expect from Evan. Some nights he was a lot of fun, the funniest, happiest guy around.

Other nights "his arm slipped." People would get hurt.

"You keep staring at that photo," Shannon said from the small loveseat.

Her words brought Meg back to the present. "Yeah. I know."

"It's a weird photo, isn't it?" Shannon asked, shaking her head. "Evan looks like some kind of Martian."

"He doesn't look like Evan," Meg said with some sadness.

They sat across from each other in silence for a long while. Finally Meg said, "You've got to forgive me, Shannon. It was temporary insanity, I guess. I really do apologize. I was out of my head. Really. I've been crazy for days. I mean, when I got home from Lisa's the other night, I saw shadows of flower pots on the porch. I was terrified! I was sure someone was waiting there to get me."

"Poor kid," Shannon said unsympathetically. "When does the groveling begin?"

"Forgive me and I'll do anything. I mean it. I'll even ask Gary Brandt to go out with you."

"You'll *what?*"

"You know you want to go out with him, but you're too shy to ask."

"Now, listen—"

"So I'll ask him for you. Really. I'll do it to make up for this afternoon."

"Good lord. I think you're serious." Shannon stared at her friend in disbelief.

"Of course I'm serious. I really don't want you to be mad at me."

"Okay. I'm not mad," Shannon said. "But don't you dare ask Gary Brandt anything."

"Okay, I—"

"Promise?"

"Promise," Meg said. She shifted in the seat, starting to feel a little relieved. "Do you really accept my apology?"

"Yeah. Sure. I overreacted a little. I'm sorry too." Shannon came over and gave Meg a quick hug. "Now tell me about these threats. I really don't believe it," she said, shaking her head.

Meg told her about the phone call, the note, and about Tony being followed. "Oh—I almost forgot. I talked to Ellen," she said, happy to change the subject. "I called her. She sounded great. Really good. She's really looking forward to coming back and seeing everyone."

"Glad to hear it," Shannon said. "I have to admit I was wrong about the party. It is a good idea. You were right."

"Good!" Meg said. "I mean *great!* So you'll help me with it and everything?"

"Yeah, sure," Shannon said with a shrug. "Why shouldn't we both risk our lives? Risk our lives for the right to party! Yeah!"

Meg laughed, but she didn't really think it was too funny.

"Oh, before I forget," Shannon said, "Mike will be

home that weekend, so we'll have to invite him even though he doesn't know Ellen very well."

Mike was Shannon's half-brother. When Shannon's mother died, her father remarried and a few years later, had Mike. Meg had seen very little of Mike. He went away to school, somewhere up in New England.

"That's good," Meg said. "Mike's real cute."

"He's gotten to look so much like Evan, it's creepy," Shannon said wistfully. "So who do you think wants to stop this party?" she asked, sighing sadly. It was a year later, but she still wanted to avoid talking about Evan.

"I just can't figure it out," Meg said, shifting her legs on the uncomfortable chair. "It's really making me crazy."

"It must be someone who really hates Ellen," Shannon said, shaking her head.

"But who could that be?" Meg asked. "Ellen was just about the most popular girl at Shadyside."

"Beats me," Shannon said. "I just haven't got a clue. Hey—maybe it doesn't have to do with Ellen. Maybe it's someone who really hates *you*." She laughed. The idea really seemed to strike her funny.

Meg was shocked. The idea had never occurred to her. "Huh? Like who?"

"I don't know. Forget it," Shannon said quickly. "Stupid idea. Someone wants to stop this party from happening. Someone wants to keep us all from getting together again. But why?"

"What is this person afraid of?" Meg asked, thinking hard. "Hmmmm . . . Afraid that we'll talk about him? Afraid that some secret will come out? Afraid that Ellen will tell us something?"

"Maybe, maybe." Shannon was tapping her fingers nervously on the antique coffee table. "Now who might have a secret they wouldn't want any of us to know about. . . ." Her face suddenly tightened. Her expression turned grim. "Brian!" she cried.

Meg stared back at her in surprise. "Brian?" Meg thought of her suspect list. Brian, of course, was her number one suspect. "What makes you say Brian?"

"Well . . . he's so weird, Meg. I know he's your cousin and all. But he's so weird. And he's gotten so much weirder ever since . . . ever since that day. Didn't you ever wonder what Brian was doing in the woods, how he just happened to find Evan seconds after—after . . ." She couldn't finish her thought.

"Shannon, you don't think Brian had anything to do with—"

Shannon stared into Meg's eyes. "It's possible, isn't it?"

"Yes, but—" Meg knew Brian was weird. And she had always thought it a coincidence that he had come upon Ellen and Evan just after Evan had accidentally shot himself. But in typical naive fashion, Meg had never suspected that Brian might have had something to do with Evan's death.

"I guess I should go confront Brian," Meg said.

"Try to be a little more subtle than you were with me," Shannon said pointedly.

Both girls laughed. Meg was very glad she had come over. Now maybe she could go home and be able to concentrate on her psych paper.

She said good night to Shannon, walked out the front door and down the long drive, and began jogging over the wet pavement toward home. She realized it must have rained again while she was at Shannon's, for the street was very wet and currents of water were rolling down the curbsides toward the storm drains.

She looked up and saw car headlights and then a dark car behind them. It was coming toward her very fast, its tires splashing up waves of rainwater on both sides as it moved.

Keeping to the curb, Meg continued to jog. But she froze in place when she realized that the car had swerved so that it was coming right at her.

It seemed to speed up.

She had no time to move, no time to jump out of its path.

Frozen like a frightened deer, she tossed up her hands as if to shield herself, and screamed as the car roared down on her.

chapter
9

*T*he driver pulled the car to the curb in front of the house and shifted into park. His heart seemed to be pounding in rhythm with the windshield wipers. *Thump-THUMP Thump-THUMP Thump-THUMP.*

He turned off the engine. The wipers came to an abrupt stop in the middle of the windshield, but his heart kept up the insistent rhythm. He didn't make a move to get out of the car. He didn't know if he could walk. He stared out the windshield, waiting to feel better, waiting to feel a little calmer, a little more normal.

Maybe he'd never feel normal again.

The rain had stopped completely. It had been a fast, hard storm and had blown over in a minute.

Where was he?

He looked around. It took a while to remember. He was in front of his cousin Mark's house. He was sitting in Mark's car. He had borrowed the car that morning.

He was returning it when he had seen Meg jogging in the street. And then . . . and then . . .

He ran Meg down.

No, he didn't.

But he nearly had.

What had he been thinking of? What happened to his brain? He realized he was sweating now. The sweat was rolling down his forehead. His T-shirt was drenched. He felt hot all over, hotter than he'd ever felt.

What had happened to his brain?

The windshield was steaming up. Soon he'd be wrapped in this safe cocoon. No one could see him. No one could know he was in there. Maybe he'd stay in there forever.

He had nearly run Meg down. He had aimed the car right at her, and then he had floored it.

He heard her scream over the roar of the engine.

He saw her eyes go wild.

He saw her shield herself with her hands. Still he kept the gas pedal down to the floor. Still he didn't swerve the wheel.

Then he saw her leap to the side, falling hard to the pavement.

Finally he had cut the wheel, squealed to the left. He remembered struggling to regain control. Working the wheel till the car was headed back on the road. Then he sped away. He never even looked back.

Maybe he would never feel normal again.

He had only meant to frighten Meg.

That was all. Really scare her. Show her that he meant business, that he wasn't going to kid around with any more scary phone calls, or notes, or lunch-bags filled with fake blood.

But then when he saw her in the street, he forgot what he was doing. He remembered why he had to frighten her. Oh yes. He remembered why he couldn't allow the party to take place. Yes, yes, yes.

But he forgot what he was doing, forgot his foot so heavy on the gas, forgot his hands so rigid on the wheel.

He could have killed her. He only wanted to frighten her.

He had killed once. Now he had almost killed again.

I'm losing it, he thought. I'm losing it bad.

But he had been lucky this time. She had leapt away. She was safe. She was okay.

But was she frightened?

Maybe she was frightened enough to give up the party. Then things could go back to normal—right?

Then he could feel normal again.

He'd just have the other murder to think about. Every day. For the rest of his life.

He slammed his head angrily against the side window.

No. Get control, man. Get control.

Now the left side of his head ached. Good. That felt more normal. A headache made it feel a little more normal.

Take it easy, man. Deep breaths. Yeah, that's better.

You only scared her, after all.

You have to scare her, scare her out of having this party.

You have no choice. You can't let this party take

place. You can't let everyone be all together again. You can't let Ellen come back and tell . . .

You can't let her tell what happened last year. . . .

Meg tore off the soaked, mud-stained clothes and tossed them in a heap in the middle of her bedroom floor. Then she hurried to take a hot shower.

Aside from a bruise on her shoulder where she had landed on the curbside, she was fine. Now if only she could get her hands to stop shaking, her heartbeat to slow down, her legs to stop trembling.

A nice, long shower would do the trick. She was so glad her parents had gone to bed early. She didn't really want to explain why she had returned home looking as if she had taken a swan dive into a mud puddle.

How *could* she explain it?

She wasn't sure she knew what had happened herself.

Should she call the police?

And tell them what?

She hadn't really seen the car behind the headlights. She couldn't describe it at all. It had been too dark— and then suddenly it had been too bright as the headlights bore down on her.

But had the car really swerved to hit her? Or had the driver just lost control for a moment?

The street was very slippery because of the sudden downpour just before she left Shannon's house. Maybe the driver was sliding on the street. Maybe whoever it was hadn't seen her at all. Maybe she was making a big deal over nothing.

Nothing?

She had almost been killed.

She shivered. The hot, streaming water wasn't warming her.

She dried quickly, still shivering, and pulled on her warmest flannel pajamas. Then she gathered up the clothes she had tossed onto the floor and put them down the laundry chute.

"What will make me feel better?"

Tony.

Tony would know the right things to say. Tony would know how to calm her down.

She missed Tony so much. She needed Tony now.

She pulled a pink cotton robe over the pajamas and sat down to phone him. She looked up to see a half moon peering through her window. The sky had cleared.

She punched Tony's number. It rang twice, three times, then a few more.

"Come on, Tony. Where are you?"

" 'Lo?"

"Tony?"

"No. This is his fa-father."

She recognized Mr. Colavito's muffled stammer. It meant he had spent the evening at the corner tavern. Big surprise. He spent *every* evening at the corner tavern.

"It's me, Meg, Mr. Colavito."

"M-Meg?" He sounded as if he were trying to remember if he'd ever heard that name before.

"Yes. Meg. Is Tony home?"

"No. Not now."

"He isn't?"

"No. He went somewhere, I think."

Very good. Helpful, as usual. "Oh. I see. Well . . . thanks. Sorry I woke you up."

"That's okay. I was only sleeping."

Meg hung up. Tony's dad had been drinking even more than usual lately. Tony didn't talk about it much. But she knew it worried him.

She stared at the phone. Where could Tony be so late on a school night?

She sent out a mental signal: "Tony—I need you. Call me. Call me, Tony. Are you getting this message?" She concentrated hard, giving full force to any telepathic powers she might have.

Then an unhappy thought interrupted her message-sending.

He couldn't be out with someone else, could he?

Could he?

Tony, walking quickly, did not pick up Meg's telepathic signal. He was six blocks from his home on the Canyon Road. His sneakers were soaked, as were the cuffs of his jeans. He must have walked through rain puddles without noticing them. He couldn't wait to get home and change into some dry clothes.

The street was silent except for the sound of water dripping off the tall trees and the damp sound of his shoes against the pavement as he walked.

Suddenly he heard a loud, insistent thumping sound. Tony automatically felt his chest. But the sound was coming from the driveway of a house halfway down the block. White spotlights attached to the roof lit up the entire drive and side of the house. It's almost as bright as day over there, Tony marveled.

He kept walking till he recognized the guy shooting

baskets on a brightly lit garage backboard. It was Brian's *Wizards & Dungeons* buddy. "Hey—Dwayne!"

Dwayne Colligan didn't look up. He dribbled in for a layup, missed, took the rebound, and dribbled back down the drive. "I thought I smelled you in the neighborhood, Colavito" was his cheerful greeting.

Tony ran across the neighbor's lawn onto Dwayne's drive, waited for his moment, and stole the ball from Dwayne. "Hey, Tony—you'll infect my ball, man!"

"Take a lesson, Colligan," Tony said and made a high hook shot. Swish. It didn't even touch the rim.

"Lucky shot," Dwayne scoffed.

"What are you doing out here in the middle of the night?" Tony asked, looking up at the bright spotlights.

"I like to shoot baskets at night, man," Dwayne said, dribbling in and making an easy layup. "It's kinda soothing, you know." He caught his own rebound and quickly shot again, this time a fade-away hook shot. "Where you comin' from, Tony?"

"Around," Tony said.

Dwayne dribbled in circles around Tony. His biceps flexed when he dribbled. He had powerful arms. His body didn't look like a teenager's. He had spent thousands of hours getting it that way.

"So how's it going?" Tony asked, just making conversation as Dwayne missed an easy jumpshot.

"It's going," Dwayne said with a shrug. He grabbed the rebound and dribbled away from Tony.

"How's it going with Shannon?" Tony asked, grinning.

"Not great," Dwayne said, very serious. He tossed

up a wild shot that bounced off the side of the garage. "Truth is, she won't go out with me."

"That's a downer, man," Tony said, chasing the ball down the drive.

"I don't get it," Dwayne said, pushing both hands against the shingled wall of the house and doing some quick stretching exercises. "I know her brother hated me."

"Evan?"

"He hated my guts. He told me to stay away from his sister. He knew I was hot for her. He said he'd make me regret it if I ever came near her."

"Yeah?" Tony dribbled the ball hard against the asphalt drive. He never knew any of this. Evan had never talked about Dwayne to him.

"You know something, man," Dwayne said, a wide smile on his pale face, "when they found Evan shot dead in the woods, that was good news to me. I was glad. That meant I could go get his sister."

Tony felt the rage start in his chest, then spread over his entire body.

"Evan was my best friend!"

He screamed so loud, he hurt his throat.

He pulled back the basketball in one hand and heaved it with all his might, slamming it into Dwayne's stomach.

Dwayne uttered a groan of surprise. Tony started to run, slipping on the wet driveway. He was three houses away when Dwayne called after him. "What's your problem, dork?" he shouted. But he made no move to come after Tony.

Tony kept running, picking up speed as he ran.

"You're a real dork, man!" Dwayne shouted, cradling the ball against his stomach with both of his big, meaty hands. "What's wrong with you, anyway?!"

Tony ran for two blocks before stopping. Now he was drenched with sweat. But he felt much better.

In fact, he felt pretty good.

He didn't like people saying bad things about Evan. In fact, he wouldn't stand for it.

Evan was a great guy.

Dwayne was a first-class sleazoid creep.

He couldn't stand there and let someone like Dwayne say he was glad that Evan was dead. He had to throw the basketball at him. He had to hurt Dwayne for saying that. He had to do something—and he did.

Tony felt good about that. He felt so good, he ran the rest of the way home, four long blocks without slowing down once.

chapter
10

*M*eg knew she was in big trouble over her psych paper now. It was already three days overdue. She had written only two paragraphs, and she wasn't sure she liked them.

But what could she do? She had so much on her mind.

If only she could talk to Tony, tell him what had been going on, tell him about the lunchbag filled with fake blood, tell him about the car that tried to run her down . . . maybe.

She had looked for him in school. But he wasn't there.

She threw her pen down and crinkled up the sheet of notebook paper she had been staring at. I should be with Tony right now, she thought. It's Friday night. I shouldn't be sitting here alone, writing a boring paper.

What was Tony trying to prove, anyway? That he was as stubborn as she was? Why hadn't he called her?

She jumped up from her desk. "I'm going over there," she said aloud. "Right now."

She told her parents she was going over to Tony's, took the car keys from their usual shelf by the door, and drove to the end of the Canyon Road to the small rowhouse where Tony and his father lived.

Thinking of all she had to say to Tony, imagining how they would make up, she parked against the curb and ran up the steps to Tony's front stoop.

The door swung open before she could knock. Tony's father stepped out, the Cubs cap he always wore pulled down low on his forehead. He looked as surprised to see her as she was to see him. She was always surprised by how much he looked like Tony, a slighter, gray-haired version.

"Hi. How are you?" they both said at once.

"I was just going out for a . . . uh . . . walk," Mr. Colavito said. That meant he was heading to the corner tavern.

"Is Tony home?"

"No."

"No?"

"No. Sorry. Anything I can do? You okay?"

"Yeah. I'm . . . okay. Do you know where he went?"

Mr. Colavito started down the steps. Meg stayed at his side. Somewhere down the street, a cat was screeching its head off. It started all the dogs in the neighborhood barking, an animal symphony.

"He went with that boy Brian. He's your cousin, ain't he?"

"Brian. Yeah. Tony went somewhere with Brian?"

Since when would Tony have anything to do with Brian?

"Yeah. They went off to play some kind of game together." Mr. Colavito walked quickly. He was eager to get to the tavern.

"Wizards and Dungeons?"

"Yeah. That's it. I think that's it. Tony said not to worry. He wouldn't be out too late. You can try callin' him later." He hurried on ahead.

"Okay. Thanks," Meg called after him. "Did they say where they were going?"

"Nope. They didn't tell me," Tony's dad called back, and disappeared around the corner.

Meg slowly climbed back into her car, feeling more confused than ever. Tony wasn't into *Wizards & Dungeons*. And he never could stand Brian. Why on earth would he suddenly go off on a Friday night with Brian to play the game?

Did they go to the Fear Street woods? That was where Brian and Dwayne always went to play it. Would he really go to those frightening woods with Brian, after all that had happened there?

Meg thought she might drive around for a while, but she suddenly felt very tired. She drove straight home, pulled the car up the drive, ran inside, and went up to bed.

It took more than an hour to get to sleep. When she finally did manage to drift off, she had strange, colorful dreams, troubling dreams in which she was chasing people, chasing the wrong people, chasing people she didn't even know.

The ringing phone on her desk woke her up. For a

long moment she thought she was still dreaming. Still chasing. Still being chased.

She picked up the receiver reluctantly. "Hello?" Sleep clogged her throat.

"Hello, Meg? Are Brian and Tony there?"

"No. Who is this?"

"It's Tony's dad."

"Oh. Hi. Sorry. I was asleep. I—"

"They're not there?" He sounded strange, very tense. He spoke too clearly, too distinctly, as if he'd been drinking and was trying to hide it.

"No. Of course not."

"It's four in the morning," Mr. Colavito said. "Brian's mother called me. Brian isn't home and neither is Tony. Do you have any idea where they might have gone to play that stupid game?"

"Well . . . uh . . . I don't know. The Fear Street woods, maybe . . ." Meg forced herself to wake up. What was going on here? Why did Mr. Colavito sound so worried?

"I'm calling the police," he told her. "Tony and Brian have both disappeared."

chapter
11

*M*eg was wide awake now. Too awake. Her mind filled with horrifying images of Tony and Brian, of the thick, dreaded woods where so many tragedies, explained and unexplained, had taken place.

Tony, what were you doing there? she thought. Why were you in those woods with Brian tonight?

And why haven't you come out?

She knew she had to go there. She had to see that they were all right. She crept over to her closet and pulled out the jeans she had been wearing earlier. Struggling to pull them up in the dark, she stumbled, bumped her desk, and the desk lamp went crashing to the floor.

"What was that?" she heard her mother ask in the next room.

A few seconds later her father lumbered out to investigate, turning on the hall light and peering into her room.

"Meg—where are you going? What time is it?" He

looked like a bear coming out of hibernation, yawning and squinting at her.

"It's late, Dad. But I have to go out."

"Where are you going?" he repeated, rubbing his thick, black stubble. He looked very confused.

"Uh . . . well . . . Tony's missing, you see."

"Missing? What do you mean missing? Where?"

"In the Fear Street woods, I think."

Her father thought about that for a while. Meg pulled a heavy wool sweater down over her head. She had it all the way on before she realized it was backward. She decided to leave it that way.

"Let me get this straight. You're going to the Fear Street woods?" Her father was starting to wake up.

"Yes. I have to. Tony and Brian went there, I think, earlier this evening. Now they're missing."

"Fear Street?" He was trying hard to make sense of what Meg was telling him. But of course it didn't make any sense at all. "Sorry. I'm not letting you go there in the middle of the night."

"But, Tony—Dad, please—I have to! Brian once showed me the cave where he goes to play *Wizards and Dungeons*. I think I can find it. The police won't know where it is. I can help them."

He thought about it, rubbing his dark stubble. "Oh, all right. But I'll have to go with you. Just give me a second." He disappeared back into the bedroom.

Meg stood in the hall. She could hear him explaining quickly to her mother, banging into furniture as he pulled on his clothes. She thought of running to the car, driving away before he could come after her. But something held her back. She realized she was glad he was coming.

The dangers of the Fear Street woods weren't just rumor. People really did disappear in those dark hills that stretched for miles past the end of Fear Street. Strange, impossible accidents were reported in the newspaper. Trees fell, seemingly for no reason at all. Normally fearful animals attacked with bizarre ferocity.

Perhaps the strangest thing of all about those woods was that no birds ever ventured there. No birds chewed the ripe wild berries, or dug for worms in the soft earth, or built nests in the trees. Over the years, teams of scientists from universities around the nation had come intent on explaining why the woods were bird-free. But they all went home as mystified as when they had arrived.

"Ready?" Mr. Dalton reappeared in the hallway in a heavy plaid wool shirt and corduroys. "Let me just get a couple of flashlights. You can tell me the whole story on the way."

There wasn't much to tell. As they drove down the silent, empty roads toward Fear Street, Meg told him about Tony and Brian going off to play *Wizards & Dungeons*. And then about the call she had just received from Tony's dad.

"Tony isn't into that game, is he?" her father asked, turning on the windshield wipers to remove the thick mist from the windshield.

"No," Meg answered quietly. "He isn't."

"I didn't think so. He's not the type."

Meg was too tired to ask her father what he meant by that. She knew he didn't really approve of Tony. He probably meant it as some kind of a dig. But she didn't want to get into any kind of discussion now

She just wanted to concentrate, concentrate on Tony and Brian being okay.

As they turned down Fear Street, the sky seemed to darken. Meg realized it was because of the trees that overhung the street. They passed the old cemetery and followed the narrow, curving street to its end.

Flashing red lights indicated that the police were already there. Two patrol cars were parked at the edge of the woods, the lights on their roofs blood red, circling soundlessly, a silent alarm that made Meg's heart jump and made the fear she had been holding down rise up to her throat.

She jumped out before her father stopped the car and ran across the wet ground, blinking against the harsh red lights, fighting the fear, pushing it back down so that she could breathe.

"Oh. Hi." She bumped right into Tony's dad, who leaned against a patrol car, trying to regain his balance. His eyes looked red and watery in the harsh light.

He pointed into the woods. "They're in there somewhere. The cops found footprints. They're gonna find 'em." It was obvious that he'd had quite a bit to drink. Meg had to struggle to make out what he was saying.

Brian's parents, Sid and Marge, Meg's aunt and uncle, hurried over, their faces tight with worry. "Meg, you didn't have to come," Sid said, squeezing her arm as if making sure she was really there. "I'm sure Brian and Tony are perfectly— Oh. Hi, Todd."

Meg's dad appeared behind Meg, looking grim and uncomfortable. "Any sign of 'em?"

"Not yet. But they're in there," Marge said, her voice a whisper. She looked away.

"We don't know why Brian likes that game so much," Sid said. "He probably just lost track of time. He's been doin' that a lot these days."

"That's probably it," Meg's dad said, not too convincingly. He looked over at Tony's dad, who was still propped up against one of the patrol cars, his eyes swimming in his head. Mr. Dalton frowned and then suddenly remembered the flashlights he was carrying. "Let's go. We can help the police look for them." He offered a flashlight to Brian's dad.

Sid started to take it, but Marge pulled his hand back. "No. Stay here with me. The police said to stay here by the cars, not to go hunting for them."

"I'm not just going to stand here," Mr. Dalton said impatiently. "They didn't tell that to me."

"I'm coming with you," Meg said, reaching for a flashlight. "I know where the cave is where they play. Follow me."

Mr. Dalton hesitated for a moment, pulling back on the flashlight, but, seeing the frantic look on Meg's face, he relented. "Okay. But stick close to me. Stay right with me, you hear?"

Meg nodded agreement, clicked on the flashlight, and followed its narrow beam of light into the woods. The ground was blanketed with dried, brown leaves and fallen twigs. Every footstep made a loud crunch which seemed to echo through the trees. Meg stopped, thinking someone was following them. But it was just the sound of her own sneakers crackling over the leafy ground.

"Someone's gonna have to give those boys a good talkin' to," Mr. Dalton said, aiming his flashlight at his feet but still stumbling over a fallen tree limb. He landed hard on his knees but quickly pulled himself up and continued on. "They've got no right to scare us all this way."

Meg didn't say anything. She was thinking of Evan. Then Brian. Then Brian finding Evan, shot dead in these same woods.

Meg's father wandered off to the left. She could see his flashlight flickering between the trees. Lost in her own thoughts, she didn't realize they were heading in different directions.

She shivered. The air was wet and cold. It didn't feel like spring in the woods tonight. Tree frogs began to chirp, a sudden, deafening symphony of scratching. She heard a flapping sound overhead. It wasn't a bird. It must have been a bat.

"TONY!" she shouted suddenly. Her voice didn't sound like her at all. It sounded like a frightened girl in a bad horror movie. *Nightmare on Fear Street,* she thought. Freddy's coming. Freddy's coming!

No!

Stop thinking stupid thoughts.

"TONY! TONY!" She didn't care what she sounded like. She just wanted to find him.

Something darted behind the wide trunk of an old maple tree. Something—or someone?

"TONY? BRIAN? ARE YOU THERE?"

No. It was an animal, a racoon, slinking out of her circle of light, seeking the safety of the dark.

Without thinking, she followed the creature, trying to get it back into her light. She stopped when she realized she had become sidetracked, and changed

direction, moving the yellow light in wide circles now
The tree frogs stopped their shrieking as suddenly as
they had started. Now the only sound was the crack
ling of the dry leaves beneath her sneakers and—

"Dad?"

Where was he?

She had kept his light in view in the corner of her
eye. But now she couldn't find it.

"Dad? Hey—Dad?"

No reply.

She had wandered too far, following that stupid
racoon, lost in her own morbid thoughts. And now she
was alone. At least until she could find him again. Or
until she could find Tony and Brian.

"TONY? TONY? CAN YOU HEAR ME?"

Where were the police? Where were their flashlights? How far had she wandered? What direction
was she going?

She turned around. Then turned around again.
Nothing but blackness. "TONY? BRIAN?"

She climbed a low hill, slipping on the wet leaves.
The Fear Street woods weren't flat. Low hills and
sharp ravines made hiking treacherous in the daytime.
At night, she realized, it was impossible not to stum-
ble, not to fall. "TONY? DAD?"

Silence.

I'm not going to get frightened, she thought. But
what was that tight feeling in her throat? And why did
her legs feel so rubbery? And why could she feel her
heart pounding against her chest?

No. I'm not going to get frightened. At least, not
any more frightened than I already am. "DAD?" Her

voice sounded so weak. She was trying to shout, but she couldn't. Her mouth felt so dry. "DAD? TONY?"

Where were they?

Where was she?

She took a few steps forward, then turned around. She followed her beam of light through the trees. A tall, thick clump of flowering weeds appeared to be a man leaning toward her. She turned away from it, feeling a stab of fright course down her back. She took a few more steps. But was she going forward or back? She moved the light in a circle. She was spinning. No. The ground was spinning.

STOP!

She took determined steps, careful but determined, walking in a straight line, twigs crackling loudly beneath her, another low, gray animal slinking out of the light which she kept directly ahead of her.

"TONY? DAD? ANYBODY HEAR ME?"

She stopped.

But the crackling continued for a few seconds.

She spun around. "Who is it?"

Silence.

Had she just imagined it? It sounded like footsteps.

She started walking again. A twig snapped like a gunshot behind her.

She stopped. Someone was there. "Tony? Is that you? Brian?" She swung the light around, moving it slowly in a wide arc. No one.

Was it the police? Her dad? No. They would've answered her.

Was someone else lurking in the woods—a *stranger?*

She started walking faster. The footsteps behind her

came faster. She was up on the balls of her feet, trying to tiptoe away, trying to run over the impossibly tangled ground.

But whoever pursued her was faster.

"OHHHH!"

A hand grabbed her shoulder roughly from behind.

chapter

12

*H*er flashlight was kicked from her hand. It sailed into a deep clump of leaves, its light buried. Meg tried to twist free. But the hand held tight, squeezing her shoulder harder as she struggled. She realized she was gasping for air. The sharp pain from her shoulder was spreading down her arm, down her side, down her entire body.

The grip on her shoulder tightened. She felt hot breath against her cheek. She smelled onions and french fry grease.

"I warned you—don't have the party."

The words were whispered but the whisper was a roar.

With one desperate surge of strength, she pulled herself out of the suffocating grasp. She lurched forward—and screamed as she began to fall. She raised her hands to grab onto something. But there was nothing to grab.

She was falling down a steep ravine, falling face

forward, then rolling. Her head hit something hard, a rock or a tree stump.

Lights flashed in her head, flashed in rhythm to the throbbing pain.

The lights didn't stop, even though she was unconscious.

She came to quickly, feeling the pain in her head and in her shoulder. She didn't know where she was. She looked for her ceiling, her dresser, her desk. But she wasn't in bed.

She was lying on wet ground, in a deep, foul-smelling pile of decaying leaves and weeds.

She sat up, her head throbbing harder. She remembered now.

"Hey—" She tried to shout, but she didn't make any sound. She reached up and pulled twigs from her hair.

My hair. I must look a mess, she thought.

Of all the crazy things to think about. Am I going crazy?

A leaf was stuck against the back of her neck. She pulled it away and felt a surge of nausea. She fought it back. And sitting up straight, taking deep breaths, fought back the dizziness too.

And stood up.

And saw the body lying at her feet.

At least, she saw part of a body. A sweatshirt pulled up to reveal bare skin. The back of the sweatshirt, torn and stained. Blue jeans. An arm.

Wait a minute. Was she seeing things? Was she hallucinating because of her fall?

She dropped to her knees to get a closer look. No. It was a real body. It moved suddenly, and groaned.

It was alive.

The stains on the sweatshirt. The stains . . .

She reached forward and touched the sleeve, pulling her hand back as she felt the warm wetness. Blood.

She crawled around him, and turned him so she could see the face.

Brian.

Not Tony. Brian.

She felt so guilty for thinking that. But she couldn't stop her thoughts. She couldn't hold back the feeling of relief she felt.

"Brian—are you awake? Can you hear me?"

He groaned again but didn't move. His mouth was bleeding.

She saw his face in the light. It was swollen and bloody.

The light?

Someone was shining a flashlight down on them. "Meg? What—what are you doing here?" a familiar voice called from the top of the ravine.

"Tony? Is that you? You're okay? Are you really okay?"

He came sliding down the side of the ravine. Then he ran to her, pulled her up from the ground, and put his arms around her.

"Tony—I was so worried. Oh, I'm so glad to see you! Somebody grabbed me and pushed me and—"

He held her tighter, pressing his cheek against her forehead. "Ssshhhh. It's going to be okay," he said softly.

"But, Brian—" she started. "He—he's—"

She could feel Tony's muscles go tense. He let go of her and took a step back. "I went to get help, but I got turned around. I was heading into the woods instead of to the street.''

"But what happened?" Meg cried, feeling her panic return the moment Tony let go of her.

"Brian fell down the ravine. I guess his flashlight went out and he tried to run without it. I didn't see him fall. It took me a long while to find him. Then I went to get help."

"But I don't understand why—"

"How did you find him?" Tony asked. "Meg, what are you doing here?"

"Someone grabbed me. I got away, but I fell," she said, reaching for his hand, squeezing his hand. "Oh— your hand is cut!"

He pulled it away from her. "From branches and things. I was running, trying to get help. I guess I cut myself. Who grabbed you? What happened?" He spoke to her tenderly, his face filled with concern.

He still cared about her. Despite the horror of what had just happened, she felt strangely relieved.

"I couldn't see him. It happened so fast."

"OVER HERE! HERE THEY ARE!"

"YOU KIDS OKAY?"

The shouting voices were accompanied by darting circles of light, and in a few seconds, two policemen appeared, followed by Meg's dad. "You're okay?" he cried, rushing forward to hug her. "I thought you were right with me. I turned away and you were gone."

"Where's the other one?" one of the policemen asked Tony, shining his flashlight into Tony's face. The policeman was very young, Meg saw. He looked as young as Tony, although that was impossible, and he seemed very frantic, as if this were the first excitement he'd had on the job.

Tony turned away from the harsh light and pointed down into the ravine. "Brian's down there. He fell. He's hurt pretty bad."

"Radio for an ambulance," the policeman told his partner as he scrambled down the side of the ravine to examine Brian. The other policeman turned and started to run to the patrol car.

"He's beat up pretty bad," the policeman called, squatting next to Brian, shining his light in Brian's face. The policeman sounded too upset.

Don't they teach them to always sound calm? Meg asked herself.

Brian stirred and opened his eyes. He tried to lift his head, but the policeman gently indicated for him to lie back.

"What happened here, son?" The policeman shined his light in Tony's face.

That's funny, Meg thought. He looks younger than Tony, but he calls Tony "son."

Tony squinted back at him. He looked very tired and very frightened, Meg thought. "He fell. I didn't really see it."

"Pretty bad fall," the policeman said, lowering his light to Tony's chest. The front of Tony's sweatshirt was mudstained and torn.

"I went for help," Tony told him. "But I got lost."

"What were you doing here late at night in the first place?" the policeman demanded. Meg could hear an ambulance siren in the distance.

"Nothing, really," Tony said uncomfortably. "Playing a game."

"Some game," the policeman growled. He took off his uniform jacket and draped it over Brian's chest. "Keep warm, son. You're going to be okay." Brian gazed up at him. He didn't say anything. He didn't seem to know where he was.

A few minutes later the ambulance arrived. Two men in white labcoats dropped down into the ravine and lifted Brian onto a canvas stretcher.

"I'm okay," Brian insisted. "Really. I'm okay." He stared up at Meg but didn't seem to recognize her. "I'm okay. Really." She heard him protesting as they carried him off to the ambulance.

"Your dad is waiting for you," Mr. Dalton told Tony, not bothering to hide his angry feelings. "And I'd better go talk to Sid and Marge. You boys sure caused a lot of trouble and a lot of worry tonight for no good reason."

Tony looked away and didn't say anything.

"If I were your dad, I'd ground you for life," Mr. Dalton said.

"Yeah, yeah," Tony muttered under his breath.

"What did you say to me?" Meg's dad flared.

"Now, come on, Dad," Meg said softly. "It wasn't Tony's fault. He's had a hard night, too. It must have been very frightening being lost in these woods. Give him a break."

"I tried to get help," Tony repeated.

Mr. Dalton scowled at Tony. Then his face filled with surprise as he looked at Meg closely for the first time. "What happened to you? You're covered with dirt."

"I tripped," she lied quickly, feeling her face go red. Luckily, he couldn't see it by the light of the flashlight. "That ravine is impossible to see, and it's so steep."

"Poor Brian," Tony muttered.

"Poor Brian? It's a little late for that," Mr. Dalton sputtered angrily. "It's a little late for everything. Maybe you'll think twice before going off in the woods to play a stupid, worthless game." He stomped on ahead of them, looking like an angry bear who just had a fish stolen away from him.

Meg and Tony followed behind, walking slowly. Meg took Tony's arm and leaned against him as they walked. "Why *were* you here playing the game with Brian?" she asked, whispering so her father couldn't hear their conversation.

Tony shrugged. "I don't know. It looked like it might be fun."

"But you were never interested in it before," Meg said, walking even slower, letting her father get farther ahead.

"Yeah, I was," Tony told her, sounding defensive. "I just wanted to see what it was like. But I didn't know Brian was so serious about it. As soon as we got to the woods, he sort of changed. He became a Third-Level Wizard, or whatever. He was playing a character, but he *was* the character. He's too serious. It's like he lost himself completely. It's scary."

"What character did you play?" Meg asked, holding onto his arm, stepping carefully over a fallen tree limb.

"Uh . . . a warrior, I guess. It was weird."

"The whole thing's weird. You never could stand Brian. Now all of a sudden—"

"That's not true," Tony said angrily. He stopped walking and pushed away her arm. "How many times do I have to say it? I was just curious about the game. That's all. Give me a break! You want to cross-examine someone? Go to law school!"

"I'm sorry," she said quickly, surprised by his anger. "I didn't mean anything. I've had a bad night, too, you know."

He suddenly seemed to remember that she had been grabbed by someone in the darkness. His face softened. He lowered his head. "I'm sorry too," he muttered. "So you didn't see the guy who grabbed you?"

"No. It was so dark. It happened so fast. He took away my flashlight. Then he grabbed me. Then he whispered something in my ear about the party. Then I fell down the ravine."

"He *what?* What about the party?" Tony put both hands on her shoulders to stop her. "Tell me this again."

"He said, 'I warned you about the party.' Something like that. He sounded very angry, very crazy. I was so scared. He was breathing into my ear. His breath was so hot. And he really hurt my shoulder. It still aches."

Tony looked very upset. "Do you think he followed you into the woods? Do you think he was waiting outside your house and followed you here?"

"I don't know. I don't know what to think. Last night, I was coming home from Shannon's. I think someone tried to run me over in a car. I'm frightened, Tony. I—"

"Oh no. Oh no. No no no. I'm just so glad you're okay," Tony said, pulling her close. "This is all too much, Meg. Too much. You'll forget about the party now, won't you?"

"What?"

"This is just too scary, too dangerous. You'll forget about the party, right?"

"No way," Meg said, a grim frown of determination on her face. "You don't know me very well, do you! A challenge is a challenge. I'm going to have that party for Ellen. It's the only way I can find out who is doing all this to us!"

Tony let go of her. He stood staring into her eyes, then looked away.

I love the way he's so worried about me, Meg thought.

"You look so troubled," she said. "What are you thinking?"

"That you're making a big mistake," he said, suddenly looking very scared. "You've got to think about this, Meg. Really think about it. Whoever tried to run you down, whoever grabbed you tonight—he might have been trying to show you that . . . that he might do something even worse. . . ."

chapter

13

*O*n Sunday, a balmy, hazy Sunday that felt more like summer than spring, Meg slept late, had a long, leisurely breakfast of pancakes and bacon, and then walked up to North Hills to visit Brian. It wasn't exactly her idea of how to spend a Sunday afternoon, but both of her parents had urged her, and pestered her, and repeatedly told her how much it would mean to Brian, who wasn't allowed to leave his bed because the doctors thought he might have internal injuries. So finally she gave in and decided just to get it over with.

Brian lived in an enormous white house overlooking the river. With its tall columns on both sides of the double-doored entranceway, it always reminded Meg more of a Southern plantation than a house a normal person would live in. When she was little, Meg would wander off by herself down the long, carpeted corridors, peeking into room after room, until she'd get frightened and run back to where everyone else was, usually in the front parlor or the library.

The house was too big, too creaky, too old, too . . . scary. No wonder Brian grew up to be so weird!

As Meg walked up the long, smooth driveway, lined with carefully pruned hedges, she saw a familiar blue Taurus beside the house. She saw Cory Brooks and his friend David Metcalf, coming out of the house. They weren't smiling or joking around as usual, she noticed immediately.

"Hey, Meg. Hi. How's it goin'?" Cory called. She wondered if he was glad to see her, or glad to be leaving Brian's house.

"Okay, I guess," she said.

"Lookin' good," David said.

Meg was embarrassed. She suddenly remembered she hadn't even brushed her hair. She was only going to see Brian, after all. She hadn't planned on running into anyone else.

"I heard about your lunch bag the other day," Cory said sympathetically.

"Great lunch. We didn't know you were a vampire," David said, laughing at his own joke. No one else laughed.

"It was only red paint," Meg said, making a face at David. "But it sure looked like blood."

"What a bad-news joke," Cory said.

"I'm not so sure it was a joke," Meg said, feeling a sudden chill despite the heat.

"Yeah. Lisa told me someone was trying to scare you," Cory said, shaking his head. Then his mouth dropped open and his eyes nearly popped out of his head. "Lisa! Oh no! I forgot about her! I was supposed to pick her up an hour ago!"

He started running to his car, with David following. "Hey, how's Brian doing?" Meg called after them.

"Not too good!" Cory called, starting the car while David scrambled to climb in.

"He's real quiet. And when he does talk, he doesn't make any sense," David called.

He didn't make any sense *before* his fall, Meg thought. Then she scolded herself for thinking such harsh things about her poor, injured cousin. She watched Cory speed around the circular driveway and take off toward Lisa's house, which was only a few blocks away. She watched the car until it turned a corner and, realizing she couldn't put it off any longer, went up the flagstone walk and rang the bell.

"Oh, hi, Meg. Your mom told me you were coming. Brian will be so glad to see you."

"Hi, Aunt Marge. How's he doing?"

Meg's aunt chewed her lower lip. She seemed very nervous. "Oh . . . he'll be okay, I think. He's just a little . . . distracted. The shock of the accident. You know."

"Yeah. He must be pretty shaken up," Meg said awkwardly. She didn't really know what to say. She hurried past the long, mirrored dining room, down the corridor that led to Brian's room.

"He looks worse than he feels," Brian's mother called after her.

"Thanks for the warning," Meg said. She turned and glanced back just before she reached Brian's room. Aunt Marge suddenly looked so much older.

Meg continued to Brian's bedroom door, stopped just outside it, and forced a smile to her face. She froze it there, determined to keep smiling no matter what. She had come to cheer Brian up, after all.

She knocked on the heavy, oak door and walked in. Brian looked up but didn't make an attempt to sit up.

"Brian—is that you?" she cried.

Nice going, Meg, she thought. Of all the stupid things to say! Why did I say that? Why not just walk in and say, "Yecch. Your face looks like something in a butcher shop window!" Go ahead. Tell him how horrible he looks. That'll cheer him up.

"Hi, Meg," Brian said. His voice sounded okay, but his right cheek was so swollen he couldn't move his mouth very well. He had one black eye which opened only halfway. A cut on his chin, Meg saw, had required several stitches.

"Brian, you really know how to take a fall. Maybe you should be a stuntman."

He tried to laugh, but it came out a wheeze.

"A wizard doesn't need a stuntman," he said. At least, that's what Meg thought he said. He was talking so slowly and softly, it was hard for her to hear.

"I didn't bring you candy or flowers," she said, sitting down tentatively at the foot of the queen-size bed. "I didn't think you really wanted that stuff."

He stared at her with his one good eye, but didn't reply.

"Is there anything you do want? Anything I can bring you? Your homework, maybe?" She laughed, a forced laugh, but it sounded pretty genuine.

He didn't seem to hear her. "How do I look?" he asked, his voice flat, expressionless.

"You look . . . uh . . . not great." She wasn't going to lie to him. He had mirrors. He could see for himself. "Let's put it this way—you've looked better."

He seemed to be thinking about that answer. Finally he muttered something about not having the power to change things. Meg couldn't really hear him.

"Maybe things will go better for me when school's out," he said clearly, a bit louder, still staring at her with his unswollen eye.

"You'll feel better soon," she said. "Are they giving you some kind of painkillers?"

"Yeah. I guess." He turned his head away.

"You really did it to yourself this time," Meg said, trying to sound light, but it didn't come out that way.

"Did you come here to scold me?" Brian snapped. "Very helpful."

"Sorry. I didn't mean it that way," Meg said, feeling guilty. She was always picking on him, it seemed. From the time they were little kids, she had never been able to tolerate him for more than a few seconds. But she knew she should be a little more understanding now. He really looked as if he'd been run over by a truck.

She suddenly remembered Shannon's suspicions about Brian, about that day a year ago in the Fear Street woods. Did Brian have a secret—a dark, dirty secret he had been keeping from them all these months?

"What were you and Tony doing in the woods so late at night?" she asked. She leaned forward and stared into his eyes, hoping it might encourage a direct answer from him.

But he didn't say anything. Then finally, in a far-away voice, he said, "The Warrior came and fought for his place."

"Brian, really—" Meg felt the anger rise in her again, but this time held it in check.

"But the Wizard has tricks that warriors do not know of."

"Great, Brian. Great. So you and Tony were playing *Wizards and Dungeons,* or whatever it's called?"

"The battle isn't won yet," he said mysteriously.

Meg realized she had better change the subject. Brian obviously did not want to talk about what had happened. "Are you going to get back to school in time for finals?" she asked, forcing a smile.

He didn't reply.

"The seniors are out already," she told him. "Now they just have to wait for their final grades and graduation. It's supposed to rain next Tuesday, so they may have to move the graduation into the auditorium."

Again, he didn't reply. He was staring at her now. He looked as if he were thinking hard, debating something in his mind, trying to decide whether to tell her something or not.

She decided to give him one more chance to talk about the other night. "Did you ask Tony to play the game with you, or did he ask you?"

"I will reveal everything when I reach the Fourth Level and become a full-powered Wizard," Brian said.

How annoying. She just wanted to shake him. All this stupid wizard talk.

Why wouldn't he answer her question? She really wanted to know about Friday night in the Fear Street woods. Was it Tony's idea to go play the game in the woods? Did Brian somehow force him to come along? Tony wouldn't talk about it, and neither would Brian. Why? Were they *both* afraid of something, of someone?

"You look tired, Brian. Maybe I should go." She stood up and stretched.

"Thank you," he said softly. Was it thank you for coming? Or thank you for going?

"You'll feel better real soon," she said. "You just need plenty of rest."

"Thank you," he repeated.

She reached forward and squeezed his hand. It felt soft and lifeless, like an overripe peach.

She started to leave, but he held on to her wrist. He pulled her back with surprising strength. She waited for him to explain, but he stared up at her silently.

She waited a long while, her hand gripped by his, waiting for him to speak.

"I—I should confess," he said finally, letting go of her hand.

"What?" She wasn't sure she had heard correctly. She stared down at the bedspread. It was too painful to look at his swollen, purple jaw from this close.

"I—uh . . . no." He seemed to change his mind. He turned his head toward the window.

The room darkened as clouds covered the sun. The breeze from the window had turned cold and damp. Another storm was blowing up outside.

Meg felt a chill that wasn't caused by the wind. She suddenly had a hunch. A hunch about what Brian wanted to say, about what he wanted to confess.

She took a deep breath. "Brian," she said. "Look at me."

He turned back to face her.

"Brian—did you make a call? Have you been calling me?"

"Yes," he said calmly. "I have."

chapter

14

Sunday Afternoon

"What?"

She hadn't expected him to confess so quickly, so easily. He was so casual about it, it was hard to believe him.

She waited for him to apologize, to start to explain, but he just stared back at her blankly.

The room grew darker. Nervously, she walked around the bed and clicked on the table lamp beside it. The lamp cast a yellow glow over his face, leaving his black eye and swollen jaw in shadows, making his wounds seem deeper, more ugly.

"You admit it? You made that call?" Her voice came out higher and shriller than she had wanted. But his casualness was unnerving her.

"Yes," he said, a narrow smile forming on one side of his puffy, swollen cheek. "I wanted—"

He started to add something, but they were interrupted. His father poked his head into the room, looking concerned. "Everything okay in here?"

"Yes. Fine, Uncle Sid," Meg said quickly.

"How are you feeling, Brian?" his dad asked.

"Okay," Brian said after a long pause.

"Can I get you two anything? A Coke or something? A cup of tea?"

"No. No thanks, Uncle Sid. We're fine."

He left reluctantly. Meg listened to him pad down the long corridor, then turned back to Brian. "What were you going to say? About the call?"

"Yes." Brian stared up at her with his one good eye. "Yes, I remember. I've been calling. And I think I can reach Evan."

"Evan?!"

"I have the power, Meg. I have the Fourth-Level power. I think I can call Evan back."

"Cut the crap, Brian!" Meg shouted with sudden vehemence. She stood over him, her face twisted in anger. "I asked you a straight question. I want a straight answer. You're not going to hide behind any of this phony sword and sorcery baloney! You're going to tell me the truth."

Brian suddenly looked very frightened.

He couldn't be that frightened of me, Meg thought. What is he really frightened of? She was determined to find out before she left the room. "Did you call me or not?"

"Yes, I called you," he said, looking to the window. "I called you several times, three or four, I guess."

"What? Several times? Why? Why did you do it?"

"I wanted to warn you—" He stopped. "I can't talk about it. I really can't."

"What did you want to warn me about, Brian?" She

wasn't going to back down. "What were you trying to prove?"

That seemed to make him angry. His swollen face turned scarlet. "I wasn't trying to prove anything. I told you. I was trying to warn you—"

"Of?"

"To . . . uh . . . be careful. But I couldn't tell you. I couldn't admit that . . . uh . . . I just couldn't. I hung up each time before you picked up the phone."

"What??" What was he talking about? Wasn't he confessing that he had made the threatening, whispered call, that he had been the one trying to frighten her?

"I was scared, Meg. I don't want to explain. I really can't explain. I'm telling you too much already. I can't tell you. I just can't."

"Can't tell me what, Brian? Can't admit what??"

He shook his head sadly. "You really don't understand anything, do you?"

"Can't admit what?" She felt so confused now, so frustrated. Why wouldn't he tell her what was on his mind?

"I can't, Meg. I just can't tell you. Don't try to force me. It won't do you any good. It won't do either of us any good. I'm warning you—"

"Stop saying that, Brian. Stop saying you're warning me. You're not making any sense. You're not explaining anything."

Suddenly he sat up and grabbed her wrist again. He leaned forward, pulling his swollen, battered face close to hers. Close up, in the dim bedroom light, he looked like a creature from a horror movie. The bitter, sharp aroma of antibiotic ointment rose from his face. Meg felt as if she couldn't breathe.

He pulled her even closer. "I'm warning you," he said, in a low voice she had never heard before. "There are things you don't understand. There are dangers. Real dangers. The woods . . . It wasn't an accident. . . . I mean—I can't . . . I shouldn't. But, listen to me, Meg. Watch out. I'm warning you. . . ."

He's threatening me, Meg thought.

This isn't a warning. It's a threat. But why?

He let go of her wrist and slumped back on his pillow. He suddenly looked exhausted, completely drained.

"Brian—"

He turned his back to her.

Rubbing her wrist, she silently ran out of the room, down the long, thick-carpeted corridor, and out the front door. On the front porch she stopped and leaned against one of the white columns, taking deep breaths, trying to get the smell of Brian's skin ointment out of her nose.

She looked up. Someone was walking across the porch.

"Ellen!"

"Oh!" Ellen's mouth dropped open in shock. "Meg! I didn't—"

"Ellen, what are you doing here?" Meg shrieked, completely shocked to see her.

"Well, I—uh . . ." Ellen looked really embarrassed.

"I didn't even know you were in town yet!"

"Well, yes. I . . ."

Meg ran over and gave her old friend a hug. "You look great!" she cried. She took a step back. Ellen looked exactly the same. She still looked beautiful with no makeup at all. Her hair was lighter and longer, but still tossed back simply behind her narrow shoulders. She was still so tall and lanky, still looked exactly like Daryl Hannah.

Ellen gave Meg an uncomfortable smile. "I just got in . . . a few hours ago. I was going to call you."

"I—I'm just so surprised," Meg said. "I looked up—and there you were!"

"It's really nice to see you," Ellen said stiffly, looking toward the double front doors. "How's Shannon?"

"Good. She's good," Meg said. "She can't wait to see you!"

"I'm at my aunt Amy's. Why don't you come over after school tomorrow? Bring Shannon too."

"Okay. Great!" Meg said brightly. "It's been such a long time. I can't wait to talk to you."

"Me too," Ellen said. She pulled her tan raincoat tighter and shivered. Ellen was always freezing, any time of year.

"What are you doing here?" Meg asked, suddenly remembering they were standing on Brian's front porch.

"I heard about Brian. About his accident. In the woods. I thought I'd just . . . you know . . . stop in and say hi."

"Oh. That's great," Meg said. "He can really use some cheering up. He's not in great shape."

"It must have been awful," Ellen said, closing her eyes. She stepped forward and gave Meg another hug. "See you tomorrow?"

"Can't wait. You look great. Really!"

"Thanks." Ellen turned and walked up to the front door.

Meg stepped off the porch, turned to watch Ellen go into the house, then headed for home, hurrying to beat the rain, thinking about Brian, the awful look on his face, the threats he made to her.

As soon as she got home, she rushed to her room and phoned Tony. "Please be home, Tony. Be home."

"Hello?"

"Tony? Hi. It's me."

"Meg. How are you?"

"Uh . . . I'm not sure. I was just over at Brian's."

"Yeah?" His interest seemed to perk up. "What happened? How come you sound so funny?"

"Well . . . Brian said the weirdest things to me. Frightening things. I really couldn't believe—"

"Brian what!?" Tony's voice stayed cool, but there was an edge to it.

"He said he shouldn't say anything. I mean, he wasn't going to—but he told me—"

There was a long silence at the other end. Finally, in what was almost a whisper, Tony said, "He did? He *told* you?" He suddenly sounded very upset.

"He warned me—"

"Listen—" Tony started.

"My parents are home. I've got to get off," Meg said. "We've got to talk, Tony. Later."

"Yeah," Tony agreed. "Brian told you, huh?"

"Well, yes, he—"

"We've got to talk, Meg. Tonight."

"No. I can't tonight, Tony. I've got to write my psych paper. I—"

"Okay. What about David's party tomorrow night?

We'll meet there and then go somewhere, just the two of us."

"Yeah. Okay. That would be good." Meg was pleased. Tony never wanted to talk about anything serious lately. Now, here he was, volunteering to have a real discussion, just the two of them.

"We'll go up to River Ridge. We'll take a walk up there and we'll talk," Tony said.

"River Ridge? You mean the place they call Lover's Leap?"

"It's pretty up there, and we'll be alone," Tony said softly. "We haven't been together for so long. It'll be real nice, Meg. Just the two of us."

"Okay. But isn't it dangerous up there?" Meg asked.

"I'll take care of you," Tony said.

chapter

15

*T*ony didn't realize how tightly he was gripping the phone receiver. When he slammed it down, his hand was tingling. His palm began to itch. He scratched it hard with the fingernails of his other hand, scratching faster and faster until the skin was red and raw, but the itching didn't go away.

The back of his neck felt cold and wet. He realized his legs were trembling. Still scratching his palm, he plopped down on the living room couch, threw his head back against one arm, and stared up at the ceiling.

So Brian had talked. Well, big surprise. Lately Tony had suspected that Brian might talk. He was the weakest one. Ellen's return, the plans for the party would be a perfect excuse for Brian to let go and spill his guts.

That's why Tony had done everything he could to make sure Brian wouldn't talk. Hadn't he taken Brian out to the Fear Street woods and beaten him up as a reminder not to talk?

But he talked anyway.

He *squealed*. That's the word they always used in gangster movies on TV. Brian *squealed*.

And now Meg knew.

Meg knew that Tony killed Evan. Brian had told her.

Tony uttered a loud cry, a moan of regret, of pain, of anger, and slammed his fist into the sofa cushion.

What was he going to do now?

Meg knew . . . Meg knew about last year. . . .

Once again Tony saw himself in those dreaded woods. Saw Ellen. Saw Evan.

Once again he felt the hunting rifle in his hands, Evan's rifle. Once again they struggled for control of it, screaming at each other, pulling with all their strength, out of control, out of all reason, pulling, pulling, pulling. . . .

And the gun went off. Just a loud pop. Like a firecracker, almost.

And Evan fell.

Tony had killed Evan.

And Ellen was screaming. In the background the whole time, Ellen was screaming. Like a wailing siren. Like a broken alarm. She was sitting on a fallen tree, pulling the sides of her straight, blond hair with both hands as if holding on to herself, and screaming, her eyes frozen open, staring straight ahead at Tony, staring at the boy who had just killed Evan.

But Tony hadn't meant to shoot Evan.

Or had he?

That's what he couldn't decide. What was he thinking at the moment? Was he thinking that he wanted to kill his friend, Ellen's boyfriend? Was he thinking that he *had* to kill him?

No.

It was an accident. It was just an accident. They struggled. The gun went off.

Because Tony had *wanted* it to go off.

No!

Tony *wanted* Evan dead.

No!

These thoughts were going to drive him crazy.

Maybe he already was crazy.

What was he going to do now? What was he going to do about Meg?

He didn't have a choice, did he? Meg wanted to talk to him. She didn't want to believe all that Brian had told her. That was so much like Meg. She wanted Tony to tell her that it all wasn't true, that everything was going to be just fine.

If I deny it, she'll believe me, he thought.

But that wasn't the answer. There was still Brian. And there was still Ellen. Ellen could talk. Ellen could give him away just as Brian had.

Maybe I shouldn't have beaten Brian up, he told himself, his mind going back a few nights ago to the woods, pictures of their fight in the darkness repeating behind his closed eyelids, pictures accompanied by the sound of his fist pounding Brian's chest, his shoulders, his stomach, and then his face.

Brian had told anyway. Despite Tony's fierce warning, after nearly a year of keeping the secret, Brian had told.

And now what was Tony supposed to do about Meg?

Didn't Brian realize the danger he was putting Meg in by telling her how Evan had been murdered?

No. Of course not. Brian wouldn't think of that.

What to do about Meg?

He couldn't let her turn him in. He couldn't let her tell everyone that he was a murderer. His life would be ruined. Over. All over.

He couldn't allow that.

She wouldn't keep his secret. She was such a straight arrow. There was no way he could trust her to keep the secret.

But he couldn't kill Meg, too—could he?

"No!" he said aloud. He sat up. Maybe if he sat up, the ringing in his ears would go away. Maybe his palm would stop itching.

He couldn't kill her—but he *had* to kill her. He had to push her off the River Ridge.

It was Brian's fault. Brian left Tony no choice. No choice at all.

Now it was either Meg or him.

And it wasn't going to be him. It was going to be Meg.

One push and his secret would be safe. One push. And what an excellent warning that would be to El-len—and to Brian—not to say another word. They'd get the message, okay. They'd understand that they'd be next.

But, wait. This was Meg. Meg, Meg, Meg. He loved Meg—didn't he? He cared so much about Meg. Could he really be thinking of killing her? Could he really do it, just push her over the ridge?

Was he really a cold-blooded killer?

No!

Maybe.

Meg had sounded so worried on the phone. So horrified. But not horrified enough.

How could she be so trusting? How could she agree to go with him to River Ridge? She was just such a trusting, naive person. She was stupid. No. Maybe she really didn't believe Brian. Maybe Brian told her, and she refused to believe it.

Why should she believe Brian, anyway? Everyone knew he was weird and crazy. Out in the woods all the time playing that stupid game with Dwayne.

I don't have a choice, he decided. I have to kill poor Meg. Let me count the reasons. One. She knows too much. Two. It will be a warning to Ellen and Brian. Three. If Meg is dead, the surprise party will be canceled.

No, I can't. Not Meg. Not Meg.

But I have to.

I already killed Evan, my best friend. I can kill Meg, too.

Sorry, Meg. You understand, don't you? Of course you do.

You're always so understanding.

chapter
16

"So you didn't call the police after the car tried to run you down?"

"No. Maybe I should have, but I didn't," Meg said. "I mean, what could I tell them? I didn't even get a good look at the car. It was too dark. All I saw was headlights."

"But, Meg—" Shannon started.

"Besides, now I'm not even that sure it was trying to run me down. I mean, the road was real slippery because of the rain. Maybe the driver just lost control for a second. If I call the police, they won't be able to do anything. It'll just be a waste of time."

"But what about the guy who grabbed you in the woods?"

"Same thing," Meg said. "I didn't see him or anything. There's nothing helpful I can tell the police. Don't look at me like that, Shannon. I really think calling the police would be a waste of time."

Shannon shrugged. "Whatever."

They looked up at Ellen's aunt's house. It was bright yellow with freshly painted white shutters. The front lawn sloped up sharply. To get to the house, the girls would have to climb about a hundred flagstone steps built into the sloping grass.

"We should've brought mountain-climbing gear," Shannon complained, motioning for Meg to go first. "And a Saint Bernard." She followed Meg up the crooked stairs. "You want to go to David Metcalf's party tonight? He's having an end-of-school party because his parents are out of town."

"Yeah, I know," Meg said. "I'm meeting Tony there. We can go together. Pass the oxygen, please." They were halfway up the hill.

"Gee, it'll be great to see Ellen again," Shannon said. "Of course, we'll be too winded from the climb to talk to her. We can just make hand signals."

"She looked great," Meg said, suddenly feeling nervous about seeing her old friend.

Shannon was staring straight up. Meg followed Shannon's gaze and discovered that Ellen was standing at the top of the slope, waving down at them.

"Hi!"

"Hi! Hurry up!"

"Throw us a rope!"

Ellen was wearing a sleeveless, wine-colored T-shirt and white tennis shorts that emphasized her long legs. Her hair seemed even lighter, almost silvery, in the sun.

At the top of the hill a lot of hugs were exchanged, and everyone commented with high-pitched delight on how everyone hadn't changed a bit and how wonderful

118

everyone looked and how great it was to be together again.

"Shall we go in?" Ellen asked. "My aunt is out shopping, but—"

"Let's stay out here. It's so pretty," Meg said, plopping down on the grass. "I love being able to look down the street from so high up."

"It doesn't take much to get Meg excited," Shannon cracked. She sat down on the top flagstone, straightening her blue top.

"So how are you?" Ellen asked, grinning at them both, her hair glowing in the sunlight. She took a seat between them and squeezed Meg's hand.

"Fine."

"Okay."

"How about you?"

"Yeah. Good. Real good," Ellen said. She giggled, a high-pitched giggle. Meg recognized it as her nervous giggle. When she was really tense, Meg knew, Ellen would end every sentence with that little jingle of a giggle.

They looked down the hill as a boy rode by on his bike. We were doing fine when we were standing up, Meg thought. Now it's gotten awkward. Come on, please. Somebody think of something to say.

"How's your new school?" Shannon asked Ellen.

Ellen put her hands behind her in the grass and leaned back on them. "It's okay, I guess. It's big. Much bigger than Shadyside. Sometimes I feel kinda . . . lost." The giggle again.

They stared down the hill. "What's happening at Shadyside?" Ellen asked, her fixed grin finally fading.

"Not much," Shannon said.

Meg's mind went blank. She couldn't think of any-thing interesting to tell Ellen. It's been a whole year, she thought. There must be *something!* "A few new teachers," she said. How lame.

"Cory Brooks and Lisa Blume are going together," Shannon said.

"You're kidding!" Ellen reacted with a little too much surprise, Meg thought. It wasn't *that* shocking, after all.

"That's amazing," Ellen added, followed by her nervous giggle.

"You going with anybody?" Meg blurted out. She could feel her face getting red. Sure, it was a normal question to ask someone—but not Ellen, not after her last boyfriend shot himself to death in the woods.

You're being too sensitive. That was a year ago, she scolded herself.

Ellen did look uncomfortable. "No," she said quickly, putting her grin back on her face. "I haven't really met anyone I like that much. I mean . . . I've gone out a few times. But . . ." She made a face.

"Suki Thomas got caught shoplifting," Shannon said, changing the subject.

"Big surprise," Ellen said, shaking her head.

"It was pretty serious," Meg said. "She has to see a probation officer and everything."

"That's probably made her even more popular with the boys," Ellen said. "Right?"

"Yeah, she's real popular," Meg said.

"That's because she'll do it with any boy who asks her," Shannon said.

Ellen laughed. "You still know how to cut to the nitty-gritty, Shannon."

A green flower-delivery truck rolled by down below. A small cloud drifted over the sun, casting a shadow on the grassy hill. The three girls stared at the truck, each of them trying to think of something to say next.

"There are so many things I want to ask you," Meg told Ellen. "But it's been so long, it's sort of hard to know where to start."

Ellen and Shannon quickly agreed, as if that explained away their awkwardness, their inability to talk freely and easily the way they always had.

"You still going with Tony?" Ellen asked, not looking at Meg.

"Yeah," Meg said, feeling herself blush again. Why did she feel uncomfortable about that? "We're still together. Tony's had sort of a rough time, though."

Ellen shifted her position on the grass. "Tell me about it." Bitterness creeping into her voice. She pulled out a wide blade of grass and began sucking on it, her eyes narrowing as the sun reappeared.

"It's pretty here," Shannon said.

"Yes. Very," Meg quickly agreed. This is horrible, she thought. Why can't we talk about anything?

"Shadyside seems so much smaller to me now," Ellen said, yawning. "Oh. Sorry. I stayed up till two watching a movie on cable. Do you believe we don't have cable at home?"

"How can you live without cable?" Shannon asked, brightening.

Ellen shrugged. "I took my aunt's car and went driving around. Everything looked the same, only smaller. It takes less than half an hour to drive everywhere."

"Yeah," Meg said, "Shadyside isn't exactly your

major metropolis.'' What a stupid and boring thing to say, she thought.

"You been playing any tennis?'' Shannon asked.

Ellen didn't seem to hear her.

"I miss our Saturday morning games,'' Shannon said.

"Remember the games we used to play when we were kids?'' Meg asked. How lame, she thought. When in doubt, start talking about when you were kids.

"Yeah. Remember shadow-chasing?'' Shannon said, a bit too eagerly. She was obviously pleased to have something safe to talk about. "What a dumb game that was.''

"That wasn't our dumbest game,'' Ellen said, laughing. "Our dumbest game was 'Eek, A Mouse.' ''

"I'd forgotten all about that one!'' Meg cried. "It was just a screaming contest, right? We'd pretend we saw a mouse and then see who could make the most terrifying, earth-shattering scream.''

"That was a great game,'' Shannon said. "We should play it right now. Bet I'd win.''

"Bet you wouldn't,'' Ellen said.

But they didn't play the dumb kid's game. They fumbled around, trying to think of other things to talk about for a while. Meg felt more and more awkward. She knew that the other two felt the same, which made her feel even worse.

A gray station wagon started to pull to the curb down at the bottom of the sloping yard. "There's Aunt Amy,'' Ellen said, climbing quickly to her feet and brushing off the back of her tennis shorts. "I'd better go help her with the groceries." She seemed grateful for the interruption.

"Guess we'd better get going," Shannon said, sounding dejected and not hiding it at all.

"You're . . . uh . . . still coming out for pizza with us Saturday night, right?" Meg asked, trying to sound casual. Saturday night, of course, was the surprise party. Going out for pizza was the excuse Meg and Shannon had dreamed up to get Ellen to the party.

"Yeah. Right. Great," Ellen said with forced enthusiasm. "See ya."

"See ya, Ellen."

"You look great!"

Meg and Shannon descended the flagstone steps quickly in silence. They didn't say a word to each other until they were inside Shannon's red Mazda. "Well, that was just like old times," Shannon said sarcastically.

Meg felt so bad, she thought she might cry. But she took a deep breath and held it in. The visit was so awful, she thought. It was like losing a friend all over again. "We didn't have much to say to one another," she said tentatively. She wasn't sure how Shannon felt about it all. But maybe if she talked about how she felt with Shannon she wouldn't feel so hurt, so . . . abandoned.

"Well, I guess it's natural," Shannon said. Her way of dealing with situations like this was to minimize them, act as if they were ordinary, normal, to be expected.

"I felt so bad!" Meg cried, struggling to keep herself together.

"It *was* a little awkward," Shannon admitted, her

eyes on the road. "But we haven't seen her for a whole year."

"Come on, Shannon. Admit it," Meg pleaded, shoving the seatbelt out of the way so she could lean her arms on the dashboard and rest her head on her arms. "It was dreadful. We were all totally tongue-tied and miserable."

"Aw, Meg, stop exaggerating," Shannon scolded. "It wasn't all that bad. Really. We were all nervous. But we'll get over it. And so will Ellen. I'm sure it'll go better at the party. We'll—"

"The party!" Meg wailed. "What a disaster! Why did I ever think it was a good idea? Oh, it's going to be a nightmare! Whoever's been trying to stop it was *right!*"

"Meg—"

"You think Ellen's going to be happy to be dragged to a party to see all her old friends? Shannon—she wasn't even happy to see *us!*"

"Meg—chill out. Please. You're blowing this all out of proportion. Just because we were a little nervous this afternoon doesn't mean Ellen won't like the party. It'll be completely different. We'll be different and she'll be different. You'll see. It'll be fine."

Meg just moaned with her head buried in her arms. Shannon stopped the car. "Why are you stopping?" Meg cried.

"Because you're home," Shannon said, laughing. "Get out. See you at David's party tonight."

Meg muttered some kind of good-bye and ran into the house, thinking about David's party. She realized she was really looking forward to being with Tony. It had been so long since they'd been together, just the two of them. And they had so much to talk about.

Maybe, she thought, Tony had some idea of what Brian was trying to tell her, of why Brian was threatening her. She couldn't wait to tell Tony her suspicions about Brian. Maybe Tony would be able to help her understand what was going on. . . .

chapter

17

Monday Night

"*B*et you'd never guess that David's parents are away," Shannon said, rolling her eyes.

"What a scene!" Meg said, staring out through the windshield as Shannon parked the car across from David's house.

Stereo speakers on the driveway were blaring out dance music, and couples were dancing in the garage. Kids were sprawled all over the lawn. Two couples were making out on the steps leading up to the front porch. Another couple was entwined under the tree at the side of the driveway. All of the lights in the house were on. There seemed to be even more kids inside.

Shannon climbed out of the car and slammed the door. She was wearing skin-tight white pants and a silky, wild pink top. Some guy sitting on the lawn whistled to her and called out, "Lookin' good, Shannon!" This clever remark was followed by loud appreciative laughter from the other guys on the lawn.

"Maybe we should have Ellen's party on David's

front lawn too," Shannon joked. "This looks pretty rad!"

"Let's go in the house," Meg said.

"Glad we got here early before everyone starts throwing up," Shannon said.

Walking up the drive, Meg looked for Tony, even though she knew he wouldn't be there this early.

"Think fast!" someone yelled. A basketball flew by their heads and bounced down the drive and into the street. The guys on the lawn thought that was hilarious.

"Where's David?" Shannon asked a kid they knew.

He shrugged. "Haven't seen him all night. How'd you do on the English final?"

It was Shannon's turn to shrug. Meg led the way past the couples on the front steps into the living room. The room was filled with kids from school milling about, talking and laughing. Arnie Tobin, David's friend from the gymnastics team, seemed to be asleep on the couch, probably passed out.

"This is really gross," Shannon complained. "I love it!"

"Hey—there's Lisa!" Meg cried. She waved to Lisa, who was talking to some kids by the entrance to the dining room.

"Hey, Shannon, you didn't have to dress up just for me."

Meg turned around to see who that was. It was Dwayne, a beer can in his hand, a smile on his face, as he walked up to Shannon, his dark eyes looking her up and down. He walked up very close, forcing her to take a few steps back.

"I see you dressed up too," Shannon cracked.

Dwayne was wearing a gray T-shirt, torn above one sleeve, brown stains down the front, and faded jeans with one front pocket torn off.

He stepped closer and leered down at her. He was about a foot taller than she was. "You come inside to dance with me, huh?"

"Yeah, sure. I've been dreaming about it all week," Shannon said sarcastically.

"Shall we do our dancing vertically or horizontally?" he asked, and gave a dirty laugh at his own joke.

"Dwayne—such big words for you," Shannon said. "Have you been going to night school or something?"

The smile faded from his face. His eyes went cold. "I don't like jokes like that. I'm not dumb, you know." He grabbed her arm.

"Hey—let go of me." She pulled away from him.

He laughed. "You're not scared of me, are you?"

"No. I'm not scared of garden slugs, either. I just don't want them touching me."

His face reddened as his eyes narrowed. "Give me a break, okay? I just want to dance with you. I'm not a bad guy, Shannon." He was moving forward, backing her into a corner.

"Let's get to know each other," he said, his smile returning. He wasn't looking at her face. He was staring at her tight blouse. "You'll see. I'm okay, really."

"Dwayne, please—"

"If we get along tonight, we can have an even better time at the surprise party Saturday night."

"What? What are you talking about, Dwayne? You weren't invited to that party!" Shannon shouted.

"I was, too. Suki Thomas asked me to go as her date."

Shannon's back was against the wall. Dwayne took a long sip from his can and moved in closer. "Dwayne, don't come any closer. I don't want to dance with you. I mean it."

"Don't knock it if you haven't tried it," Dwayne said with a leer.

Meg decided she'd better do something. "Hey, Shannon—Tony wants to see you!" she called. It was the first thing that came into her head. She ran over and tugged Shannon away. "He's in the kitchen. He wants to ask you something."

Dwayne shot Meg an angry look. "Tony? You mean Lunchmeat? Lunchmeat is here? Isn't this past the little boy's bedtime?"

Meg ignored him and pulled Shannon out of the corner. He started to follow. Shannon turned and flashed him a withering look. He tossed up his hands. "Oooh—the evil eye!" He laughed. "Okay, I can take a hint. Thanks for the dance. See you at the party." He tossed his empty can onto the couch. It bounced off the sleeping Arnie's stomach and rolled to the carpet. Arnie didn't stir.

"Thanks for the help. But I know how to handle that creep," Shannon told Meg. "Just hit his nose with a rolled-up newspaper."

"He's so big. He's kinda scary," Meg said.

"I'm going in the dining room. There seems to be tons of food in there," Shannon said. "You coming?"

"No. I think I'll—Oh! Here's Tony!" Tony stood at the front door, wearing straight-legged jeans and a gray leather jacket.

"Hi, Tony. Bye, Tony," Shannon said. She disappeared into the dining room.

Meg ran over to Tony. She was really glad to see him. "Hi, stranger," she said, taking his hand. His hand was ice cold.

"Great party," he said, looking around. "Where's David?"

They both saw David at the same time. He and Cory appeared in the entrance to the den, walking on their hands for some reason, their feet straight up in the air. Suddenly all of the change fell out of Cory's chinos pocket, and both boys collapsed to the floor laughing.

"Let's go," Tony said, pulling her toward the door.

"You just got here. Don't you want to talk with anyone?"

"No. Just you," he said. "Let's go where we can be alone." He smiled at her. He seemed nervous, she thought. And very pale.

A few minutes later they were in his dad's car, driving north on the River Road, heading toward River Ridge. The weather had grown cool again, and the wind gusted off the river. Meg was wearing layers of T-shirts, but she wished she had brought a jacket. "It's so dark up here," she said, snuggling close to him as he drove.

"Yeah. There aren't many lights on the River Road," he replied, staring straight ahead.

The road grew steep as it climbed toward the high ridge at the spot where the river split in two. River Ridge was actually a trail originally made by Indians. It started low on the eastern banks of the Conon. . . and followed the river, sloping up until it looked down on the water from tall, granite cliffs. The farthest and highest point of River Ridge was known as Lover's Leap. The Ridge was a romantic place to walk, especially on warm spring and summer nights, but no one really knew why that spot was called Lover's Leap.

They drove in silence for a long while. "You're very quiet tonight," Meg said finally.

"I'm just happy to be with you," he told her. His voice sounded strange to her, tight and tense. Or was she just imagining it because *she* was the tense one?

Near the top of the road, he pulled the car over and parked it between two trees. He switched off the ignition and the headlights. "Let's take a walk," he said.

"I don't have a jacket," she said, already feeling a little chilled. "Can I borrow yours?"

He hesitated. "Come on," he urged softly. "I'll keep you warm."

She got out of the car and followed him onto the path. She could hear the river flowing far below them in the darkness. The dirt path, soft beneath her sneakers, led up higher along the cliff. Tony reached back his hand and she took it.

"It's a little scary up here, don't you think?" she asked. He didn't say anything. She caught up with him and went a few steps ahead, still holding onto his hand.

"Look—we're right on the edge of the cliff," she said, suddenly alarmed. "They should put a railing or something here."

He still didn't say anything. He was standing behind her. He reached both arms around her shoulders, and, holding her tightly, guided her right up to the edge of the cliff.

chapter

18

I'll just get it over with, he thought.

It would only take a second. One hard push and over she'd go. Simple. And quick.

So why was he hesitating?

She was so trusting. She seemed so comfortable with his arms around her like that. She didn't even question him when he refused to lend her his leather jacket.

Maybe she didn't know anything after all. Maybe he was going to commit a murder he didn't have to commit.

He decided to find out. "Tell me about Brian," he said softly into her ear, leading her away from the cliff edge and a few feet onto the path.

"He was so strange," Meg said, shivering. "I didn't really understand him."

"What did he say?" Tony asked, allowing a little impatience to enter his voice.

"He said he was warning me. But it sounded like a threat."

132

"Warning you about what?"

"I don't know. He just said to be careful. He said things weren't what they seemed. He wasn't making any sense. He seemed really frightened. He told me I was in danger."

"From who? From the guy who's been trying to stop the party?" He held on to her tightly. If he had to, he could shove her over the edge from here. She'd probably be too surprised to struggle.

"I don't know. He wouldn't say."

So Brian didn't crack entirely, Tony realized. He wanted to. Brian wanted to tell her it was me. But he was too scared.

Has she figured it out? No.

"I thought maybe you could tell me what he meant," Meg said, leaning back against him.

So trustful, he thought.

"I don't know," he told her. "What else did Brian say?"

He had to push her. He decided he had to push her. Even though she hadn't figured it out, she would sooner or later. And his life would be ruined.

She was leaning back against him. One hard shove. That's all it would take. And he wouldn't have to worry—about her, anyway.

"Brian said I was in danger. That's all. He told me to be careful."

"Who did he mean?" he asked innocently. "Who was he warning you about?"

Get ready. This is it.

Push her and then run. Don't stand there listening to her scream. Don't wait to hear the splash, the sound of her body cracking as it hits the shallow river bed. Just run, Tony. You'll be okay. You'll be fine.

"I think he meant *himself*," she said uncertainly. "I was so confused. I think he was trying to warn me about *him*. But how can that be?"

Again, he hesitated. "I don't know. Brian's such a weirdo," he said.

"But how could it be Brian?" she asked. "That night in the woods, it couldn't have been Brian who grabbed me and made me fall down the ravine. Brian had already fallen into the ravine."

Is she going to put one and one together and realize that I was the only one who could have grabbed her? Tony wondered. "Then who could it have been?" he asked, preparing himself, steadying his legs, closing his eyes. He didn't really want to watch her when she went over.

"Do you think there could be two people trying to stop the party?" she asked. "Brian and someone else?"

She turned around to face him.

No. Don't turn around. Don't make it harder for me. Don't look at me now.

She has such a cute face, like a doll. So perfect. So pretty.

Don't weaken, Tony. Of course you care about her. But you care more about keeping free, keeping alive, keeping your secret . . . forever.

"Brian and someone else? I don't know." His voice trembled. He wondered if she could see how upset he was.

Please turn around. Please don't look into my eyes so lovingly.

"Tony—you weren't involved in it, were you?" Meg asked suddenly.

"What?" Tony's whole body shuddered violently.

She pressed her forehead against his cheek. "I had this dumb thought that Brian might mean you. It's so strange, the crazy things that can go through your mind when you're upset and trying to figure things out."

"Yeah. Strange," he said. "No. He couldn't mean me. No way."

She was figuring it out. Feeling her forehead against his cheek, he could almost hear her brain working, solving the mystery. Could she tell he was lying? Had she already figured out he was Evan's killer?

She pulled away. "I love the sound of the river flowing down there. It's soothing somehow."

Maybe you'd like to listen to it close up, he thought. Her voice was changing, becoming colder, becoming more suspicious. Or was he imagining that?

"I'll tell you something else kind of strange," she said. "Ellen went to see Brian. He was the first person she visited. Don't you think that's odd?"

Tony let out a short gasp. "Ellen? She—what?" He was too upset to control himself, to hide his unhappiness at this news.

He grabbed her arms. He braced his legs. He took a deep breath.

"What's wrong, Tony?" she asked softly.

"Nothing."

One hard shove. That's all it would take. She probably wouldn't even realize what was happening until she was halfway down.

No. No. No.

He wasn't going to do it.

He knew he wasn't going to do it.

I'm not a killer, he thought. I'm not a killer after all. Or was he? Could he do it?

His mind spun. For a moment he felt so dizzy he thought he might plunge over the side.

He steadied himself, holding on to Meg. What would be the point of killing Meg? She didn't know anything. She hadn't figured out anything. Killing Meg wouldn't help him in any way.

Brian was the problem. Ellen was the problem. Brian and Ellen together were the problem.

Meg was never the problem.

Okay. You get to live, Meg. And you get to have your surprise party.

He had tried to stop the party, and he had failed. But the party wasn't the problem. He had two problems. Brian and Ellen. Brian and Ellen. Brian and Ellen.

I'll be at the party with them, he thought. I'll be there with my two problems. I'll be watching them. I'll be listening to them.

He suddenly remembered the pistol his dad kept in the cabinet next to his workbench in the basement. And the box of shells next to it in the back of the shelf.

The gun. I could bring the gun. Just in case.

Yes. I'll bring the gun Saturday night.

For Brian. And Ellen.

For my own protection.

Brian already tried to give me away. Who knows what he and Ellen were cooking up together. But I'll be ready for them. I'll be ready, willing, and eager.

"Tony, what's wrong? You just had the strangest look on your face." She peered up into his eyes, her face filled with concern. For the first time he saw some suspicion there, too.

"Uh . . . nothing. Guess I'm cold. Let's go back to the car."

"But—aren't you going to kiss me first?"

Why was she looking into his eyes like that? For reassurance? For reassurance that he wasn't a murderer?

"Kiss you? Oh, yeah. Right."

He put his arms around her and kissed her, and thought about the gun waiting for him in the basement cabinet.

chapter

19

Saturday Night

*M*eg pulled the car to the curb and looked up the hill to Ellen's aunt Amy's house. A trail of tiny yellow lights went all the way up along the side of the flagstone steps to the front porch. I really don't feel like climbing those steps again, Meg thought.

She honked the horn. No sign of Ellen up there. She honked it again, longer. Why do they put such tinny horns in these foreign cars? she asked herself.

Success! Ellen appeared on the porch and signaled that she'd be down in a minute.

Meg waved back to her, grateful she didn't have to get out of the car. She felt so nervous, she wondered if she'd be able to enjoy a single moment of the party. I guess I'll feel it was worth it if it makes Ellen happy, she told herself. Meg, Shannon, and Lisa had worked all day, getting the Halsey Manor House in order, cleaning, decorating with balloons and flowers, and putting out the food and soda.

I should be looking forward to the party, she

thought. But I just know it's going to be dreadful. Ellen's going to hate it. And she's going to hate me forever. How could I have been so stupid?

But Ellen's smile as she came trotting down the steps reassured Meg. Watching Ellen descend, Meg decided the party might work out after all. Ellen had always been a good sport about everything in the old days. She was sure Ellen would be a good sport tonight. And maybe she'd even be pleased that her friends wanted to make such a fuss over her.

It was a cool and blustery night. The weather just couldn't make up its mind to stay summery. Ellen was wearing a straight, red miniskirt over black tights. And a long-sleeved black top. She looked beautiful.

I wish I were tall, Meg thought, putting on a smile as Ellen slipped into the car. Meg was wearing a turquoise, patterned Esprit sweater—her only expensive sweater—over purple pegged pants.

"Hi. Where's Shannon?"

"Oh. We're going to pick her up," Meg said, shifting into reverse so she could back away from the curb. "You look great."

"Thanks. So do you. You haven't changed a bit, Meg. You still look ten years old."

"Is that supposed to be a compliment?" Meg laughed. She headed west toward the Old Mill Road which would take them to Fear Street.

"Where are we picking up Shannon?" Ellen asked, scooting down in the seat and resting her knees on the dashboard. "At her house?" She had an apprehensive look on her face. She probably didn't want to go to Shannon's house, Meg decided. After all, it was Evan's house, too.

"No. We're picking her up at the Halsey Manor House." Meg tried her best to sound matter-of-fact about it, as if she picked Shannon up there every day of the week.

"What? That old mansion back in the woods?" Ellen was very surprised. "The Fear Street woods?"

Meg nodded, keeping her eyes on the road. She knew she was a very bad liar. She hoped Ellen wouldn't start asking her a lot of questions.

"What's she doing there?" Ellen asked, rolling down the window, deciding it was too cold, and quickly rolling it back up.

"Uh . . . I don't know. She just asked me to pick her up there." Meg decided a simple I-don't-know would get her into less trouble than making up some kind of elaborate story. "How's your aunt? Have you had a good visit?" she asked, determined to change the subject.

Ellen sighed and scooted even lower in the seat. "Oh, I don't know," she said wistfully, watching the familiar houses pass by in the darkness. "Maybe I shouldn't have come back. There are just so many memories. . . ."

Oh, wonderful, Meg thought. I'm about to drag her into a mansion full of memories!

She turned onto Fear Street, driving quickly past the cemetery and the sprawling, rundown old houses across from it. The night seemed to grow blacker the moment she turned the corner and entered Fear Street. For some reason none of the streetlights were on. And most of the houses were completely dark.

Meg saw Ellen shudder and close her eyes. They were driving past the Fear Street woods. "Oh, I hate this place," Ellen said. She opened her eyes. "We're really taking the scenic route tonight, huh?"

"I guess," Meg said. She didn't know what to say. Having the party at Shannon's would also have been a mistake. Let's face it, she told herself, having it *anywhere* is a mistake. Ellen is just not over what happened here. Maybe she never will be. And she doesn't even want to pretend that she is.

She turned down the narrow dirt road that twisted through the woods to the Halsey Manor House. She couldn't think of anything else to say to Ellen. She felt just as awkward as during their first visit on Monday. And as the headlights revealed the massive stone mansion up ahead, a feeling of dread as big and heavy as the mansion came over her.

"Frankenstein's castle," Ellen said. "I haven't been here in years. They used to have birthday parties here when we were little. Very gloomy birthday parties."

Well, welcome to another very gloomy party, Meg thought. She had an impulse to turn around in the circular drive in front of the mansion and take Ellen right back to her aunt's house. Or maybe, just keep driving, keep driving through the night until there were no familiar houses, no familiar landmarks at all . . . and no memories.

This isn't like you, Meg, she scolded herself. You always make the best of any situation. That's one of your finest qualities. This is going to be a great party once it gets going. Well, maybe not a great party—but an okay one. And Ellen will appreciate it. There's no way she won't appreciate it.

She silently thanked herself for the pep talk and

pulled the car up to the entrance to the old house. There were no other cars in sight. Everyone else had been instructed to park in back. Two stone torches bearing flickering electric lightbulbs, one much dimmer than the other, lit the doorway, which was arch-shaped and looked like a castle entrance.

"You go get her," Ellen said. "This place gives me the creeps."

Meg pulled the door handle and pushed open the door. "No. Come on in with me. Don't make me go in there alone."

Ellen frowned and pulled her legs off the dashboard. "It gives you the creeps, too, huh? What on earth can Shannon be doing in there?" She climbed out of the car and smoothed down her miniskirt. "Okay. Come on. We'll go together."

Meg felt so nervous she could barely walk. She'd never surprised anyone at a surprise party before. As she pushed open the heavy doorway and stepped into the front hallway, she vowed she'd never do it again. "After you," she told Ellen, motioning for Ellen to go in.

Their sneakers squeaked over the dark marble floor. The house was silent. An enormous, low chandelier, a confusion of brass and crystal, managed to dominate the room without providing much light.

"This way, I think," Meg said, pretending she didn't know where she was going. She led the way through the wide front chamber and pulled open a heavy door at the back. The room behind the door seemed to be dark. "In here," Meg said.

Ellen reluctantly followed her in. Meg's legs felt shaky, and she realized she was breathing really fast.

I've never been this nervous in my life, she thought. Please, please don't let this be a *total* disaster.

"SURPRISE!"

The lights came on, revealing dozens of grinning faces.

Ellen stared at Meg, not understanding what was happening.

"SURPRISE!" The cry was followed by cheers and laughter.

"Look at her!" Shannon shouted from across the room. "She really is surprised."

Meg stared at Ellen, waiting for her to smile, a smile of recognition, of acceptance, of delight.

But the smile didn't appear.

Ellen looked absolutely horrified.

chapter
20

Saturday Night

*L*ike snapshots, the scenes of the next few minutes froze in Meg's mind. Shannon hugging Ellen. Ellen finally forcing a smile to her face. Ellen hugging Lisa. Lisa laughing about how surprised Ellen looked. Ellen joking to Meg that she'd find a way to pay her back for this. Half-joking, maybe? Tony and Ellen greeting each other stiffly, each looking more uncomfortable than the other. Tony congratulating Meg for pulling the whole thing off. Kids crowding around Ellen to say hi and welcome her back. Ellen starting to look more comfortable as more kids came up to greet her.

"It's going really well!" Shannon shouted in Meg's ear, trying to be heard over the noise of the crowd.

Meg jumped. She wasn't expecting anyone to come up behind her like that. "You look great," she told Shannon.

"Doesn't Ellen look great? She really was surprised." Shannon wandered off to talk to some other

144

kids. Meg went over to Tony, who was on the edge of the crowd, not talking to anyone. "It's so hot in here. Why don't you take off that heavy leather jacket?" she asked.

"I'm okay," he said, looking annoyed. The jacket bulged out above his waist. He kept both hands in his pockets.

"Doesn't Ellen look great?" Meg said, starting to feel a lot better about the party.

"Yeah. I guess."

"You in a bad mood or something? This is supposed to be a party." Why was she giving Tony a hard time? Just nerves, she figured. She'd gotten through the surprise part of the party, but the evening still had a long way to go.

"Give me a break," he muttered. "You know I don't like parties much."

She impulsively kissed him on the cheek. "Dance with me later?"

"Maybe." He forced a half smile.

After everyone had had a chance to greet Ellen, the large room got very noisy. With school just out, everyone was in a mood to celebrate.

Lisa was chattering animatedly to Ellen, gesturing with her hands and laughing. But Ellen, seemingly distracted, kept looking over Lisa's shoulder. Meg followed Ellen's eyes. Ellen was looking at Tony.

Tony stared back at her, scowled, then looked away.

What's his problem? Meg thought. Then someone called her to help find the paper plates, and she forgot all about it.

When she looked back a few minutes later, Ellen was talking animatedly to a large group of friends.

Lisa and Cory were in the center of the room, actually getting along for once. A few feet away from them, Suki Thomas, her peroxide-blond hair spiked in angry punk style, had her arm around Dwayne's waist as Dwayne looked anxiously around the room, probably searching for Shannon. The vast room echoed with laughter and loud voices. All in all, this was a pretty terrific party, Meg decided.

"Quick—crank up some music!" Shannon shouted, startling Meg from behind once again. "And crank it all the way up! This party is *okay!*"

Meg had borrowed Tony's boom box for music. It was nearly as big as her stereo at home. She rushed across the room to put in a tape, but Ellen stopped her in the middle of the room. "Great party, Meg," Ellen said, giving Meg a hug. "What a surprise. I'm a little . . . overwhelmed."

"I thought maybe you'd be furious at me," Meg said, giggling. She had borrowed Ellen's nervous giggle, she realized.

"It was very sweet," Ellen said. "I really don't deserve it."

"Don't be silly," Meg said. "We all wanted to welcome you back. We miss you, Ellen. I do, especially."

"I miss you, too." Was that a tear in Ellen's eye? Meg couldn't believe it. It wasn't at all like Ellen to get that emotional. The party must have really touched her.

"I'm going to put some music on," Meg called to her, hurrying across the room.

Dwayne stepped in her way. She nearly ran right into him. "You seen Shannon?" he asked.

"Not lately," she said coldly. She looked for Suki and spotted her across the room, her arm around some other boy's waist.

"Tell her I'm looking for her, okay?"

"Sure, Dwayne." She hurried away from him. At the table with the boom box, she quickly shuffled through the tapes and grabbed the hottest, loudest dance music she could find, and shoved it into the player.

A few seconds later the music blasted out. It sounded great, booming off the walls and ceiling of the cavernous room. Several couples began to dance. Meg looked for Tony, but couldn't find him. Finally she spotted him sitting on the floor by himself in a corner, sipping a can of soda.

"Want to dance?" she shouted, standing over him, moving with the music.

"Maybe later," he said. He took a long swig from the can and stared past her at Ellen across the room. He still hadn't taken off his leather jacket, Meg saw, despite the heat of the room.

"Great party," Lisa said, stepping between them and giving Meg a hug. "You really did it!"

"*We* really did it!" Meg said happily. "I think we all deserve a—"

She never finished her sentence. A commotion over by the boom box in the corner caught her eye. The music stopped in mid-note. Someone screamed. The few kids who were dancing turned around, confused.

"Hey—what's going on?"

"BRIAN!"

Meg and Shannon started to run toward him. Brian was standing between the boom box table and the doorway. He had white bandages wrapped around part of his head.

"It's the return of the mummy!" someone shouted. A few kids laughed.

"QUIET, EVERYONE!" Brian screamed over the laughter.

"Brian, what are you doing here?" Meg cried.

Through his bandages she could see that his eyes were wild. He had a twisted, gleeful smile on his face. He raised both arms high in the air to signal for quiet.

"Brian, please—" Meg shouted. He didn't seem to hear her.

'What's wrong with him?" Ellen asked, coming up to Meg, a very worried look on her face. "What's he going to do?"

"Listen to the words of a Fourth-Level Wizard!" Brian shouted, his arms still high above his bandaged head.

The huge room grew absolutely silent. No one moved.

"I have the power now! I have reached the Fourth Level! And tonight, I am going to bring Evan back!"

"NO!" Ellen screamed, her mouth dropping into a wide O of horror. She tugged at the sides of her long, blond hair with both hands.

"I'll stop him!" Tony yelled, starting toward Brian, one hand clenched in a tight fist, the other reaching inside his leather jacket.

"No, wait—" Meg held Tony back.

"I am going to bring Evan back—*now!*" Brian shouted. He lowered his arms and then used both hands to point to the door.

The door slowly started to open.

"What is he *doing?*" Shannon cried. "Why is he doing this?"

"No. Stop this!" Tony called, pulling away from Meg to rush at Brian.

The door swung open. Someone was standing in the dim light of the corridor.

Someone walked slowly into the room.

"Is this a joke?" Shannon cried. "Some sort of sick joke?"

Tony froze, his hand inside his jacket.

Brian continued to point, his eyes wild with triumph, as the tall figure stepped into the light.

Some kids gasped. Some screamed.

The figure who stepped into the light was Evan.

chapter

21

Saturday Night

"NO! IT'S NOT YOU!" Tony screamed.

Evan glared at Tony. His eyes looked white in the harsh light. He pointed a finger at Tony, an accusing finger, and took a step toward him.

"NO! YOU'RE DEAD!" Tony screamed, his features twisted in panic. He pulled his hand out from under his jacket. He was gripping a large black pistol. He swung it wildly, the nose pointed up to the ceiling. "I KNOW YOU'RE DEAD BECAUSE—"

Evan took another step toward Tony.

"Tony—the gun—" Meg cried. "Where did you—why?—"

"Okay, okay!" Tony shrieked, staring into Evan's eyes. "I know why you're here, Evan! I'll tell. I'll tell everyone the whole story! I'll tell everyone who killed you!"

"Mike! Why are you doing this?" Shannon shouted. She turned to Tony. "It's not Evan—it's my half-brother Mike! For God's sake, put away the gun!"

I don't know what he's doing, but I've got to get that gun away from him before he does something horrible, Meg thought. She stumbled forward and made a desperate grab for it. But Tony pulled away from her. He shoved her away hard, raising the gun out of her reach, then pointed it at Mike.

"Okay, okay. I'll tell everything!" Tony cried. "That's what you want, isn't it? Well, all right. Listen, everyone! I know who killed Evan. I'll tell the whole story now. I—"

The lights went out.

Shouts and screams echoed off the walls. Kids were running in panic toward the door. Meg searched blindly for Tony. She wanted to grab him, hold him, take the gun away, find out what was going on, why he was so terrified, why he was about to confess.

Confess?

Yes. Tony was about to confess.

Meg felt herself begin to tremble. She thought of Brian's warning to her. And she realized that Brian and Mike must have cooked up this whole scene.

Just to frighten Tony. . . .

A gunshot just inches away from her made her jump and cry out. Someone screamed in pain. Chairs toppled over as kids tried to scramble blindly out of the pitch-black room.

"NO—PLEASE!" Now it was Meg's turn to scream. "Turn on the lights! Somebody—turn on the lights!"

A few seconds later the lights came back on. Meg looked down. She was standing over Tony. He was curled on the floor, his eyes bugged out in fear, his hand grasping his shoulder. Blood poured down his arm onto the carpet beneath him.

"Tony—"

"I—I've been shot!" He didn't seem to believe it. "I've been shot!" he repeated incredulously.

"Somebody stop him!" a girl's voice shouted.

Stop who?

Meg looked up. Who was that running to the door? It was all happening so quickly, she wasn't sure she was seeing correctly. But she was. It was Dwayne. And he had Tony's gun in his hand.

"Stop him! He shot Tony!"

Dwayne tripped over a folding chair and sailed over it, landing on his stomach on the floor. Still gripping Tony's pistol, he turned quickly and threatened everyone with it. He climbed slowly to his feet, his dark eyes darting back and forth, keeping everyone in view.

"I almost got away," he said. "I'm sorry you turned on the lights."

"Dwayne—why did you shoot Tony?" Meg screamed.

Tony, writhing on the floor, moaned and held his shoulder as his blood continued to flow in a widening circle beneath him.

"Shut up! Just shut up!" Dwayne shouted at her, aiming the gun at Meg. She could see that he was desperately trying to decide what to do next. His plan had obviously been to shoot Tony and then escape in the darkness. But now every person in the room had seen him trying to run away with the gun in his hand.

Why? Why did Dwayne shoot Tony? Why did Tony

come to the party with a gun? Meg was as confused as she was frightened.

"I've got no choice," Dwayne said, his eyes still nervously surveying everyone around the large room. "I don't want anybody comin' after me."

He moved forward quickly and grabbed Ellen roughly by the arm. He held the nose of the pistol to her temple. "You come with me. You're the likely candidate, aren't you? You helped to kill Evan too."

Meg didn't think she heard correctly. Ellen help to kill Evan? Ellen *too?* What did Dwayne mean?

"No—please—" Ellen begged.

But Dwayne dragged her to the door, the pistol pressed tightly to her forehead. "Anybody comes after me, and she's history!" Dwayne shouted. No one moved. There was no doubt in anyone's mind that Dwayne meant it.

"Please—listen to him!" Ellen cried to everyone.

Someone has to stop him, Meg thought. We can't let him take Ellen. He's already shot Tony. We can't let him shoot Ellen too.

This is all my fault. My fault. My party. My fault.

She knew she wasn't thinking clearly. She was too frightened to think clearly. But she knew she had to do something. She moved quickly along the wall, keeping in the shadows.

Dwayne didn't see her as he backed toward the door. If she could get to the door first, maybe she could surprise him, maybe she could grab the gun away, at least give Ellen a chance to run away.

Kids were standing in small groups, frozen in fear. Meg moved quickly behind them, keeping low, praying that Dwayne wouldn't see her.

Could she get to him before he got out the door? Could she startle him, surprise him enough to free Ellen?

Her head was spinning. The floor seemed to buckle beneath her feet. The walls tilted. But she kept moving steadily, silently to the door.

"That's it. Nobody move. Don't force me to do something I'd hate to do," Dwayne called. He had his arm around Ellen's waist now as he dragged her across the room. He took the gun away from her head and gestured with it, aiming it around the room as a final warning to anyone who might think of following him.

Meg got to the door first.

She took a deep breath. Dwayne was just a few feet away, backing toward her. The gun was in reach.

She could just reach out and—

He spun around. He saw her.

He shoved Ellen to the floor as Meg made her move.

Meg lunged for the gun. She saw his face. She saw his eyes.

She knew she was too late.

Dwayne caught her arm and spun her around. He slammed her hard against the wall and shoved the pistol against her neck.

He pushed the gun against her throat until Meg cried out in pain. "Let's go, babes. You're comin' too. I always wanted to have two girlfriends!"

Everything seemed speeded up now. Everything went too fast to see, too fast to think about, too fast to understand.

They were in the dark corridor. The three of them. Dwayne pushing the two girls ahead of him, threatening them with the pistol if they hesitated or slowed down. Now they were running. Running too fast.

Ellen stared straight ahead, her face a blank. Was she pretending this wasn't happening? Meg tried to stop, tried to resist, but Dwayne forced her on, shoving the gun to the back of her neck. The metal was cold, so cold. It sent shivers down her back, shivers that didn't stop when he took the gun away, shivers that made it hard to run, hard to move, hard to breathe.

He pushed them toward the front door of the old house, stopped, stood there without opening it, and then pulled them roughly back the other way. Ellen stared hard at the door. For a second Meg thought she was going to try to make a run for it. But Ellen lowered her head and closed her eyes, resigned, waiting for Dwayne to tell her where to go next.

"They'll look for us outside," he said, sounding calm, sounding cold, as cold as the pistol against Meg's back. "So we'll stay inside."

Keeping them right in front of him, he pushed them to the stairs that led down to the basement. Meg stumbled, started to fall forward, but he grabbed her arm and kept her moving. "They'll search the woods all night. But we'll be cozy and safe down here. Me and my two girlfriends. Real cozy." He laughed. He sounded very pleased with his plan.

"Why?" Meg managed to ask. Her voice came out choked and small.

"Keep moving," he ordered, giving her a hard shove that almost sent her sprawling down the tiled stairs.

"Why?" she repeated, too frightened to stop moving, too frightened to resist, too confused not to ask why. "Why did you shoot Tony?"

"I had to. I didn't know how much that stupid moron knew. But I couldn't take the chance. I couldn't let him tell everyone—"

"Tell everyone *what?*"

"That I killed Evan."

chapter

22

Saturday Night

"*B*ut Tony killed Evan!" Ellen cried. "I saw him!"

Meg stopped and uttered a cry of shock, of horror. "Tony? What are you saying, Ellen?"

"Tony killed Evan," Ellen repeated.

"That's impossible—" Meg started.

"Meg, you don't know anything," Ellen said bitterly.

"Keep moving," Dwayne ordered, gesturing with the pistol.

Where were they? He had pushed them into an area of the house that hadn't been renovated, through endless dark rooms, rooms filled with covered furniture, rooms caked with years of dust, empty rooms, rooms filled with strange tools and equipment.

They pushed open another door and stumbled into another room. Dwayne found the light switch and turned it on. It was a large kitchen. Cobwebbed and dust-covered, it appeared to have been abandoned for a very long time. Grimy copper pans hung on hooks just above their heads. A grease-stained range stood against the wall. Wooden counters were cluttered with dishes and pots that hadn't been used for years. The entire room smelled of mold and mildew and decay.

"Perfect," Dwayne said, looking around. "I like to hang around a warm, inviting kitchen. Don't you?" He laughed to himself. "Ol' Dwayne has done it again. They'll never find us here. We'll hang out a bit, get cozy, and when the excitement dies down, we'll make our escape." He gestured for the girls to sit on the floor beside the range, which they did.

He pointed the pistol at each of them and pretended to shoot them one at a time, making gun noises with his lips.

"Great sense of humor, Dwayne," Ellen muttered.

"Shut up," Dwayne said, and laughed, as if he had just cracked a joke.

"What do you think you're doing?" Ellen demanded. "I saw Tony kill Evan. Why did you go berserk up there? What is in your crazy brain?"

"You never figured out the truth?" Dwayne looked sincerely shocked.

"I *know* the truth," Ellen insisted. "I was there. Tony and I followed Evan into the Fear Street woods. We were worried about him. I had just told Evan I wanted to break up with him."

"You *what?*" Meg cried. None of this made any sense to her. Ellen break up with Evan?

"I'm sorry, Meg. I'm real sorry," Ellen said, seeing the confusion on Meg's face. "But you've got to grow up sometime, kiddo. Tony and I were going out behind your back. I wanted to go with Tony. So I told Evan."

"You and Tony?" Meg tried to keep her voice steady, but this was all too much.

"Yeah. Me and Tony. Well, you can imagine how Evan took the news. He threw a fit. He went bananas. He grabbed his father's hunting rifle and bombed off to the woods. He said he just wanted to shoot something. Anything. Well, Tony and I followed him. We were worried about him. He was so crazy. We wanted to try to calm him down. But the first thing we knew, Tony and Evan were fighting, fighting over the rifle. It went off and . . . Evan was dead. Tony killed Evan."

"I don't believe it," Meg said, feeling dazed. She pulled up her knees and curled up, resting her head against them. "Tony was there? That can't be! Brian said—"

"Brian came running up a minute or so after Tony shot Evan. He found Tony and me there, trying to decide what to do. He was scared out of his mind. He said he had it all figured out. He was going to make it look like Evan shot himself, like it was an accident. Then he threatened Brian and me. He said he'd kill us both if we ever told anyone that he was in the woods with us. Brian and I saw the look on Tony's face. We knew that he meant it."

"I—I don't believe this. I just don't," Meg insisted.

"You might as well hear the rest," Ellen said. "Tony ran off after making it look like an accident. I— I was hysterical. I couldn't think straight. I was so frightened. So was Brian. As soon as Tony was gone, we went for help. All of these months Brian and I kept our secret. That Tony killed Evan. All of these months we were too frightened to talk."

"No wonder Tony's been so weird all year," Meg said.

Dwayne laughed. Meg looked up. She had almost forgotten that he was there, standing over them with the pistol. Why was he laughing? What could possibly be so funny?

"Hey, let's give a little credit where credit is due," he said.

"What are you talking about, Dwayne?" Ellen asked.

"I thought Tony found out the truth. I thought he was going to tell it all upstairs when that Evan clone showed up. I thought he was going to tell everyone that I did it. That I did Evan." He laughed and shook his head. "I guess the joke's on Tony. That stupid moron."

He started pacing the room, twirling the pistol in his hand.

"How could you kill Evan?" Ellen persisted. "How? I saw Tony and Evan fight over the rifle. I saw Evan fall. I saw him die."

Dwayne shook his head. "You're stupid too. Tony didn't kill Evan. I did. Brain and I were playing *Wizards and Dungeons* in the woods when we heard a gunshot. Brian said we had to go see what it was. I said no. I told Brain I was going home. Brian went to see what the shot was. I followed him, keeping behind so he wouldn't see me."

"So you were there too?" Ellen cried.

"I watched everything. The whole scene. I thought Tony had killed Evan. But after he ran off, and after you and Brian went to get help, I went up close and took a look. Evan wasn't dead. He wasn't even hit.

He had hit his head on a rock and was knocked unconscious."

"Oh, no," Ellen moaned. "Evan was alive. And you—"

Dwayne nodded his head. "I hated Evan. I always hated Evan. He wouldn't let me go out with his sister. He wouldn't even let me talk to her. I wasn't good enough for her. He always made me feel like a worm. So . . . here was my chance. I picked up the rifle. And taught Evan a lesson. A final lesson. He was dead already, right? At least three other people thought so. So . . . I just made it official."

"That's the most cold-blooded thing I've ever heard," Meg cried. She realized she was trembling. Her mouth was so dry, she thought she might choke. Her hands and feet were freezing cold.

Dwayne giggled, a sick, high-pitched giggle. "Yeah, it is, ain't it!" he said boastfully. "Funny thing is, it was so easy. And kind of fun, in a way."

He'll kill us next, Meg realized. He killed Evan as easily as swatting a fly. He's laughing about it, not the least bit sorry. He shot Tony upstairs. And now we have to be next. He's told us too much. We know everything.

We're not getting out of here alive.

Dwayne grinned down at her. It was as if he could read her thoughts. He twirled the pistol menacingly and stared at them both.

I've got to do something, Meg thought. I can't just sit here. I've got to at least try to get us out of here.

"How could you kill somebody like that?" Ellen screamed at Dwayne, her voice filled with disgust, with loathing—and with new fear.

"Like this." He pointed the pistol at her and pulled back the hammer.

"No, don't—" Ellen raised her hands as if to shield herself.

Dwayne laughed and made a shooting noise again with his lips.

He isn't always going to pretend to shoot us, Meg thought. One of these times—very soon—he's going to pull the trigger for real.

"Can we stand up?" Meg asked. "My legs are falling asleep."

"Yeah. Sure," Dwayne said, still staring at Ellen. "Whatever." He twirled the pistol and dropped it. It clattered against the hard concrete floor.

Meg helped pull Ellen to her feet. And as Dwayne bent over to retrieve his pistol, she whispered in Ellen's ear, "Eek! A Mouse."

Dwayne grabbed the gun and turned back to them quickly. "You two are pretty slow," he said with a pleased sneer. "You could have made a run for it just now."

"We're not going anywhere," Meg said dispiritedly.

She wondered if Ellen had heard her. She wondered if Ellen understood. She didn't dare look at her to see. Dwayne was watching them too closely.

She just knew she had to do something. Killing Evan was so easy, Dwayne had said. She didn't want to make it easy for him. She didn't want to die in this filthy, abandoned cellar kitchen.

Her back pressed tightly against the cold tile wall, she moved an inch closer to Ellen and gave her arm a light tap. Your turn, Ellen. Remember the game? Eek,

A Mouse. Did you hear what I whispered? Please, Ellen.

Please.

"What's going on?" Dwayne shouted suddenly, raising the pistol.

"YAAAAAIIIII!" Ellen screamed at the top of her lungs, a deafening scream of pure terror, and pointed behind Dwayne. "A MOUSE!"

Startled, Dwayne turned.

Meg knew she had an instant. Less than an instant.

She reached up and grabbed a big, copper frying pan off the wall. It was heavier than she had imagined. But she didn't think about that.

In one motion she grabbed for it, reached it, pulled it down.

And as Dwayne turned back to them, she swung it.

And hit him hard in the face.

So hard the frying pan clanged, metal against bone.

Dwayne didn't utter a sound.

His eyes closed. Two teeth dropped out of his mouth. Blood gushed from both nostrils.

And he fell.

Meg picked the gun up from the floor. "Let's get upstairs," she said, breathing hard, so hard. But breathing. Grateful to be breathing. "Someone upstairs must have called the police by now."

They took a final look at Dwayne, lying face down in a dark pool of blood. Then they ran out of the dank kitchen and headed through the maze of dark, empty rooms toward the stairs.

"Hey!" Ellen called, struggling to keep up with Meg. "You sure know how to throw a party!"

chapter
23

Sunday Afternoon

"So it was Tony the whole time trying to stop the party?" Shannon tossed a pair of socks across the room to Mike, who dropped them into his suitcase. Shannon and Meg were up in Mike's room, helping him pack to go back to school.

"Yeah, it was Tony," Meg said, shaking her head. "What an idiot I was."

"You weren't an idiot," Shannon said quickly. "You were . . . uh . . ."

"Trusting," Mike said helpfully. He folded a pair of jeans into the suitcase.

"That's just another word for *idiot*," Meg said.

"Meg, please—that doesn't sound like you," Shannon said. "You've been through a horrible time. We all have. But you can't let it make you . . . uh . . ."

"Bitter," Mike said. He always liked finishing Shannon's sentences for her.

"I—I guess I've learned a lot from all this." Meg sighed wearily.

164

"Is Tony going to be okay?" Shannon asked.

"He lost a lot of blood, but the ambulance arrived quickly last night. They got him to the hospital in time. The doctors there said he'll be okay," Meg said quietly. That part of her life was over, she knew. She was so used to Tony. She wondered what it was going to be like without him now.

Shannon held up a pair of dirty sweatsocks. "You're not going to pack these, are you, Mike?"

"No. I was going to give them to you. Happy birthday."

Shannon tossed them into the suitcase. "They don't smell any worse than the rest of your clothes."

"I talked to Tony's dad," Meg said. "He's going to get him help. You know, to get his head straight. Some friends know a really good shrink in New York. Poor Tony's very mixed up. It's going to take a long time."

"Think of what a year Tony must have had," Mike said, shaking his head. "He went a whole year thinking he had killed Evan, a whole year scared to death that people would find out, scared to death his life was ruined forever. And then it turns out he didn't kill Evan after all. That's pretty heavy."

"Poor Tony. And poor Ellen," Shannon said. "And poor Brian. Poor everyone."

"Where is Ellen?" Mike asked.

"Went back home this morning," Meg told him. "I wonder when we'll ever see her again."

They were all silent for a while, each thinking about the horrifying scene the night before at the party. Bright sunlight filtered through the curtains, which fluttered in a warm breeze. Baby robins chirped from a nest just beyond the window.

"Your cousin Brian's quite a guy," Mike said finally. "When he came to me with that idea about pretending to be Evan, I thought he was nuts."

"We all thought he was nuts," Meg said. "Poor Brian. He was just so frightened of Tony. He lost himself in that fantasy game world of his just so he wouldn't have to face the real world."

"But if it wasn't for Brian and Ellen, we might never have known the truth," Mike said wistfully.

"Brian and Ellen?" Meg asked, surprised.

"Yeah. They cooked up the idea together for me to appear at the party as Evan," Mike said.

"That's why Ellen went to visit Brian!" Meg realized. "To plan that little scene."

"So Ellen knew all about the surprise party," Shannon said.

"Brian told her," Mike said. "They both couldn't stand the guilt any longer," Mike said. "They had to let the truth out. They had to let everyone know about Tony, about them, about what really happened in the Fear Street woods. They had wanted to go to the police for months. But they had waited so long, they weren't sure the police would believe them.

"And they were so frightened of Tony. They thought they'd be safer if they exposed him in front of everyone," Mike continued.

"Brian put on a really convincing crazy act," Meg said.

"He was really brave," Mike said, slamming the suitcase shut.

"You were brave too," Meg told him. She turned away. She suddenly had tears in her eyes. It was all starting to catch up to her.

Shannon came around to where Meg was sitting on the bed and put an arm around her shoulder. "You'll be okay," she said tenderly. "We'll all be okay now."

Meg wiped away the tears with the back of her hand. She and Shannon accompanied Mike down the stairs.

He stopped in the front hall and put his suitcase down. "Please go tell Dad I'm ready to go to the airport," he told Shannon.

"Aye, aye, sir." She hurried to the backyard.

He turned to Meg and smiled. "You know, I'll be back in July," he said. "Maybe we could go out or something."

Meg returned his smile. "That would be nice," she said. "I'd like to go out with you, Mike. Only . . . uh . . . one thing . . ."

"What's that?"

"Please—*no parties!*"

WATCH OUT FOR

THE OVERNIGHT

Della thought an overnight on Fear Island
would be fun. But it's no fun at all when
Della gets lost in the woods,
and the handsome stranger appears,
whispering threats,
and finally driving *her* to violence.

Suddenly she and her friends are prisoners
in a conspiracy of silence, trying to conceal the
terrible truth. But someone saw what Della did.
And he's threatening them all, forcing them back
to Fear Island
to face its nightmares again!